JEALOUS LIES

Sandra raised her hand. "I nominate Jean West," she said. Scattered applause broke out across the room, and three or four girls seconded Jean at the same time.

Sandra barely heard the rest of the meeting. She knew they would all be meeting again the next day after school to plan the first big event of the pledge season. Since she had nominated Jean, Sandra would be appointed her "sponsor." It would be up to Sandra to keep Jean up to date on all the pledge-season events and help her out in any way she could.

But Sandra had other plans. She was going to be Jean's sponsor, all right. But she was going to do everything she could to make sure that Jean didn't last through the pledge period. She was going to keep Jean out of Pi Beta Alpha—no matter what it took.

Bantam Books in the Sweet Valley High Series
Ask your bookseller for the books you have missed

SWEET VALLEY HIGH

JEALOUS LIES

Written by
Kate William

Created by
FRANCINE PASCAL

BANTAM BOOKS
TORONTO • NEW YORK • LONDON • SYDNEY • AUCKLAND

RL 6, IL age 12 and up

JEALOUS LIES
A Bantam Book / September 1986

Sweet Valley High is a trademark of Francine Pascal

Conceived by Francine Pascal

Produced by Cloverdale Press, Inc.

Cover art by James Mathewuse

ISBN 0-553-25816-8

Published simultaneously in the United States and Canada

PRINTED IN THE UNITED STATES OF AMERICA

O   0 9 8 7 6 5 4 3 2

JEALOUS LIES

One

"Listen, girls," Alice Wakefield said, her blue eyes twinkling as she glanced from one twin daughter to the other across the breakfast table. "Your brother's coming home for a whole week this coming Friday, and I want your help planning something to make his visit really special."

As Jessica helped herself to another serving of scrambled eggs, she said, "I wouldn't worry about Steve, Mom. From the way Cara's been talking, we'll be lucky if we get to see him at all!"

Cara Walker was in the junior class at Sweet Valley High with the twins and had been dating their older brother for some time now. Steven was a freshman at college and lately had been so busy with his studies that he had not been able to come home often. Jessica knew Cara had been looking forward to his vacation for ages.

"Mom's right, though, Jess," Elizabeth protested. "Don't worry," she said to her mother. "Jessica and I will think of something. You can count on us!"

Ned Wakefield's eyes crinkled up with laughter as he listened to this exchange. "Something tells me I've heard that line before," he joked. "Just keep it tame, you two. Your aged parents can't stand all the excitement you two can."

Jessica giggled. "Come on, Daddy! Liz and I keep you two young!"

Elizabeth couldn't help but agree. Despite his long hours as an attorney, her father didn't look that much older than Steven. His thick, dark hair showed no sign of gray, and his eyes sparkled with youthful enthusiasm. An interior designer, the twins' mother worked hard at her career, too. With her soft blond hair, shining blue eyes, and trim figure, she was often mistaken for the twins' older sister.

"Hey, Liz, what are you daydreaming about this time?" Jessica demanded. "I asked you if you're finished with your tea."

Elizabeth smiled and shook her head. "You go ahead, Jess," she said. She knew her sister was impatient to leave the table so she could get ready for the sorority meeting at her friend

Lila Fowler's house that afternoon, whereas Elizabeth enjoyed dawdling over Sunday brunch with her parents—just another way in which the two of them were not so identical, Elizabeth reminded herself, watching Jessica spread her bagel thickly with cream cheese.

From their physical appearance it was hard to tell the twins apart, even for the people who were closest to them. They were both sixteen years old, though Elizabeth occasionally reminded Jessica that she was four minutes older. Five·feet six inches tall, they were model-slim, with sun-streaked blond hair shimmering to their shoulders and dark-lashed, turquoise-colored eyes. They even wore identical lavaliere necklaces, presents from their parents on their last birthday.

But that was the end of "identical" as far as the twins were concerned. In everything else—friends, hobbies, tastes—they were completely different. Elizabeth was careful about everything. She liked her friends to be thoughtful, honest, and dependable; and she tried hard to live up to those virtues herself. She was an earnest student who worked especially hard in English, her favorite subject. One day Elizabeth hoped to be a writer, and in the meantime she was getting all the experience she could, writing the "Eyes and Ears" column for *The Oracle*, Sweet Valley High's newspaper.

Jessica, on the other hand, was as impetuous as her twin was cautious. She moved from one friend or hobby to another with lightning speed—not because she was fickle, but because she loved excitement. Wherever the action was, Jessica was bound to be in the midst of it. School for Jessica was a place to socialize more than a place to study, and she was always teasing Elizabeth for slaving in the *Oracle* office when she could be at the beach or doing something fun, such as cheerleading!

Take Pi Beta Alpha, for example. Jessica had convinced Elizabeth they should join the elite sorority. After they had pledged, Elizabeth had become a member in name only, while Jessica had thrown herself into the various activities of the group and was now president.

"You're coming to Lila's this afternoon, aren't you?" Jessica asked her sister anxiously, suddenly afraid her twin might be crazy enough to miss the most important meeting of the semester.

Elizabeth laughed. "Yes, I'm coming," she said. "But I can't stay very long. Enid and I are planning to go to the beach, so we're going to leave early."

Jessica shook her head sadly. She found Elizabeth's best friend, Enid Rollins, unbearably dull. "This meeting is really important, Liz," she reminded her. "We're nominating new pledges today."

"Pledges?" Mr. Wakefield said blankly. "Am I missing something?"

"For the sorority, Daddy," Jessica told him. "I'm putting Amy Sutton up. Will you second her, Liz?"

Elizabeth laughed. She and Amy Sutton had been best friends before Amy's family moved to Connecticut when Amy was at the end of sixth grade. When Amy moved back to town, Elizabeth had been incredibly excited at the prospect of resuming their friendship. But four years had proved to be filled with changes, and she discovered, to her disappointment, that Amy was very different from the friend she remembered. Obsessed with boys and her own image, she struck Elizabeth as vain and self-centered. Elizabeth didn't foresee Amy having any problem gaining admittance to the sorority, especially since Jessica was backing her nomination. "Something tells me Amy will have no shortage of supporters," she said lightly, winking at her father.

"I wonder who else will make it this time," Jessica mused.

"I just hope you girls remember to be considerate of other people's feelings," Mrs. Wakefield said. "I imagine that getting cut must be extremely painful."

Jessica looked horrified. "We have to be

selective, Mom. If Pi Beta started taking just *any-one*, our reputation would completely fall apart!"

"Yes." Mr. Wakefield chuckled as he wiped his mouth with his napkin. "I believe that the whole point of having a club is to keep people *out*."

"Daddy," Jessica protested, pouting, "it isn't like that at all." She looked quickly at Elizabeth for support. "Tell them it isn't, Liz."

Elizabeth laughed. "Well, there's a grain of truth in what Daddy says, Jess." She frowned, thinking back to the time that Robin Wilson had tried to get into the sorority. That was a long time ago, before Robin lost weight and became co-captain of the cheerleading squad with Jessica. Back then Robin was awkward and un-gainly. Jessica and some of the other girls in the sorority did all they could to keep her from getting in, and it had hurt the girl terribly. That was history now, but Elizabeth hoped nothing similar would happen with this new round of pledges. She knew most of the girls in Pi Beta Alpha were well-meaning, but the potential to hurt someone was quite strong.

"Well, don't forget about your brother with all this sorority stuff going on," Mrs. Wakefield said, beginning to clear the table.

Jessica's aqua eyes widened incredulously. "We couldn't possibly, Mom," she said. "Don't

6

you remember? Cara's in Pi Beta, too. And all Cara talks about anymore is Steven."

"We'll think of a special treat for him, Mom," Elizabeth promised, giving her mother an impulsive hug as she got up from the table.

Personally, she was looking forward to Steve's visit a million times more than the sorority pledge period. And she was beginning to think she should have skipped that afternoon's meeting altogether and convinced Enid to go straight to the beach!

"OK," Lila Fowler said, clearing her throat as she got to her feet in front of the group of girls assembled in the Fowlers' magnificent, oak-paneled recreation room. "Cut the gossip, you guys. We've got to get down to business, or we're going to be here forever." From the efficient tone in her voice, it was obvious that Lila was taking her role as pledge chairman very seriously.

Sandra Bacon was sitting toward the back of the room, looking around her with amazement. She had only been to the Fowlers' house a few times before, and each time she marveled at the size and splendor of the rooms. Lila's father was one of the richest men in the Valley. His computer firm had earned him a fortune, and judging by the grand style of his home and the grounds of Fowler Crest, it was obvious he liked to show his money off. Lila's parents were divorced, and she had no brothers and sisters, so she was the sole recipient of her father's lavish gifts. Unbelievable, Sandra thought, shaking her head and watching Lila take out a pad of paper as she tried to get the meeting under way. Lila was pretty enough, with long, light brown hair and big brown eyes. But what people noticed about her first were her designer clothes and expensive jewelry. Sandra frowned as she looked down at her own jeans and simple polo shirt.

Not that anyone would comment on the way Sandra was dressed. She knew she looked OK, as she always did. "OK," the perfect word to describe her, Sandra thought. Average height, average build, average grades. Sandra looked at the pretty, chattering, self-confident girls around her. *I've got to be the most average girl in this room.* She didn't mean to put herself down; she felt she was just being honest.

The way Sandra saw it, she was the sort of girl people liked but never really remembered. Usually people met her with a group and didn't pay that much attention to her.

Especially not when she was with Jean.

Jean West had been Sandra's best friend for as long as she could remember. They had grown up together, sharing absolutely everything:

records, games, clothes. Jeanie had two brothers, and Sandra had three, but neither had a sister. And that was what they'd been like to each other for years and years—sisters. But Sandra was getting sick of living in Jean's shadow. The trouble with doing everything with Jean West was that Jean was spectacular at every single thing she did. Put spectacular next to average, and average looked a whole lot worse.

OK, Sandra thought morosely, *so Jeanie can't help the fact that she was born with the kind of looks she's got.* Long, glossy, dark brown hair, big green eyes and perfect white skin. She was petite and had a perfect figure. Jean never had to worry about gaining weight. She had a fast metabolism, she was always saying, so she could eat anything she wanted and still stay slim. And her clothes . . . everything she wore was original—and perfect. Unlike most of her classmates, Jean never wore jeans. She usually wore skirts or dresses, and she looked just that much more sophisticated than anybody else—just that much more glamorous. For years Sandra had never given Jean's appearance a second thought. Then all of a sudden, wherever they went, people told Jean how terrific she looked. And no one said anything to Sandra.

But that wasn't all. Jean did *everything* perfectly. Take cheerleading, for example. Sandra had made the squad by the skin of her teeth, stumbling during one of the jumps and struggling to look natural. She had to work very hard to learn the routines. Jean, on the other hand, made even the most complex routine look simple. And she was that way at everything! Where Sandra got B's, Jean got A's; she played the flute and had won award after award; she was a fabulous dancer; and she was even a great cook!

Sandra had never been able to tell Jean how she felt. She just knew that things had been getting worse lately. Once she had started comparing herself to Jean, she just couldn't stop.

There was only one thing in the world Sandra had that Jean didn't. That was Pi Beta Alpha. And Sandra was bound and determined to make sure Jean stayed out of the sorority.

"Sandy!" Cara Walker exclaimed, plopping down in the seat beside her. "I'm late," she said apologetically. "Have I missed anything important?"

Sandra shook her head. "Lila's about to start taking nominations. You haven't missed a thing."

"Good," Cara said, her brown eyes shining. "I was just talking to Jessica. She's putting Amy Sutton up."

"Really?" Sandra said. Her mouth felt dry. She knew everyone expected her to nominate

Jean. Jean had been too busy with a special music project to go through the last pledge period, but she was perfect Pi Beta Alpha material. Everyone had been saying so to Sandra for weeks. They all wanted Jean to get in.

More important, Jean wanted to join the sorority. She had asked Sandra about it several times, but Sandra had always managed to brush her off.

She couldn't tell anyone the truth; they'd think she was horrible. Jean was her best friend, and she knew her feelings were wrong. She was being disloyal to the girl she cared about most in the world.

But Sandra was convinced once Jean got into Pi Beta, their friendship would collapse. She felt that the sorority was the only thing that set her apart, that made Jean respect her. Once Jean joined . . .

Sandra blinked back tears. She couldn't let anyone see how upset she was. They were counting on her to nominate Jean, and she had already decided she would have to go ahead and do it. Everyone would wonder what was wrong if she didn't, and word would get back to Jean.

No, the thing to do was to go ahead as if everything were normal. But after that . . .

"OK," Lila said. "Nominations are officially open. Who'd like to start?"

Jessica's hand shot up. "I nominate Amy Sutton," she said.

"And I second her!" Cara said enthusiastically.

Sandra raised her hand. "I nominate Jeanie West," she said. Scattered applause broke out across the room, and three or four girls seconded Jean at the same time.

Sandra barely heard the rest of the meeting. She knew they would all be meeting again the next day after school to plan the first big event of the pledge season. Since she had nominated Jean, Sandra would be appointed her "sponsor." It would be up to Sandra to keep Jean up to date on all the pledge-season events and help her out in any way she could.

But Sandra had other plans. She was going to be Jean's sponsor, all right. But she was going to do everything she could to insure that Jean didn't make it through the pledge period. She was going to keep Jean out of Pi Beta Alpha—no matter what it took.

Two

"So tell me what happened at the meeting yesterday," Jean said, dangling her legs in the blue-green water of the Sweet Valley High swimming pool. It was Monday morning, and the girls were practicing water-ballet routines. Sandra looked glumly at Jean's sleek black tank suit. Only Jean West could look great in one of those things, she grumbled to herself. Her own suit felt a size too small, and her only consolation was that water ballet wasn't co-ed. She would die if a boy saw her looking like this!

"I told you," she said. "We nominated people and seconded them, and that was it. I think this afternoon we'll actually start planning the pledge events."

Jean shivered. "I hope there's nothing too

terrible," she said. "Sandra, I'll just die if I don't make it!"

Sandra looked down at the water. "I'm sure you won't have any problems," she said, trying to sound casual. "They're all pretty easy things. Of course," she added, "the first time you mess up an assignment, you're out. That's the rule. But don't worry. You'll sail through."

Jean bit her lip. "Sandy, you're making me nervous. What sort of things will they be?"

"Oh, you know," Sandra said, waving her hand vaguely in the air. "Just silly things." She looked thoughtfully at her friend. "I don't know if we're going to do what we did last time, but if we do, someone will have a party this Saturday night, and each pledge will be given an assignment of a guy to bring as her date."

Jean paled. "That's awful," she said. "What if the guy finds out?"

Sandra laughed. "Well, you've got to arrange things so he doesn't. Don't worry," she added quickly. "Honestly, Jean, you'll do fine. Can you imagine a single guy in this school who wouldn't jump at a chance to be your date?" She watched Jean's face carefully for a clue.

Jean frowned. "I'm sure there are tons of guys who'd say no to me," she said. "You're just being generous, Sandy. You always say really nice things to me."

"Well, like I said, don't worry about a thing." Sandra slipped down into the water. "I'd better get to work on my water ballet. I still can't get this routine right."

"Let me help you," Jean said, slipping in beside her and pulling her cap down over her ears. "All you have to do is keep your hands really close to you, and move them really quickly—and keep your legs straight when you kick, like this."

Sandra watched Jean flip onto her back and propel herself through the water, her legs kicking up a froth of spray. When she was a few yards away, she stopped kicking, paused for four beats, and did a perfect somersault in the water. She went through the entire routine as gracefully as if she had been doing it for months, even though, she had learned it only a few days before.

It wasn't fair, Sandra thought, diving down and coming up with a noseful of chlorinated water. Why was Jean so darned good at *everything*?

She had no idea how she was going to keep her friend from getting through the pledge season with the effortless skill that seemed to be hers naturally. The only thing Sandra could think of was to arrange to get Jean assigned to a guy who would be sure to turn her down for Saturday night. She was fairly certain a party of some sort would be arranged and that there would be a dating assignment; it was a Pi Beta tradition by now.

But who *wouldn't* want to go to a party with Jean? Sandra remembered how amused everyone had been when Jessica had suggested that Robin Wilson take Bruce Patman to a big school dance. Bruce was one of the richest, best-looking guys in the school, and at that time he was also the snobbiest.

But Jean was hardly Robin Wilson. And no matter how hard Sandra tried to think of an impossible date for her, she kept drawing a blank.

She hated to admit it, but she was beginning to be afraid she was going to have to give up.

"Winston, what are you doing?" Elizabeth complained with an amused smile. Winston Egbert was the acknowledged clown of the junior class, and he viewed lunchtime as an opportunity to play pranks. That day he was making what he called "lovegrams," paper airplanes with secret messages in them, which he sailed across the cafeteria in the direction of the girl they were meant for.

"This one's for Lila." Winston grinned and aimed the paper plane carefully, watching with satisfaction as it glided into her lap. Lila turned around with a grimace, mouthing something unintelligible at Winston.

Sandra giggled. "You really ought to market some of your ideas, Winston. You're wasting your talent around this place."

Winston smiled. "The world isn't ready for my ingenious devices," he said immodestly. "Want me to fly one of these babies to someone for you, Sandy?"

Sandra shook her head. "No, thanks," she said. She was too busy worrying about Jean and Pi Beta Alpha to let herself be sidetracked.

"Listen, you two," Elizabeth said. "I want to throw a surprise party for my brother next week. Do you think you can come?"

"My calendar is empty," Winston said. "I'm all yours, Liz."

Elizabeth smiled. "What about you, Sandy? And Jeanie, too, if she can make it. I was thinking of having it on Saturday, the fourteenth, 'cause we're having a big Friday the Thirteenth dance the night before in the gym."

"That's right," Sandra said. "I completely forgot about that. It sounds fun, Liz. I'd love to come."

"Where's Jeanie now?" Winston asked her. "I thought you two were inseparable."

"She's making up a French test. We don't do *everything* together, Winston."

Winston shrugged. "I don't even know Jeanie. She's kind of hard to get to know, isn't she?"

Sandra frowned. However complex her own feelings were for her friend these days, she couldn't stand hearing Jean criticized. "What do you mean?" she said sharply. "Jeanie's the sweetest, friendliest girl in school."

"I don't want to start an argument, but not everyone seems to feel that way," Winston said.

Sandra stared at him. "What do you mean?"

Winston shrugged. "Nothing important. I just ran into Tom McKay, looking kind of glum this morning, and he said he had tried to talk to Jeanie this morning and she really gave him the brush-off. He was good and mad, to tell you the truth."

Sandra looked at Winston thoughtfully. Tom McKay. She had never thought about him before. He wouldn't be bad as a candidate for an impossible date, especially judging from what Winston had just said. She got to her feet, her eyes bright.

"Hey, don't leave," Winston said, looking concerned. "I didn't mean to get you upset, Sandy."

"It's OK, Winston," Sandra said. "I just remembered something I forgot to tell Lila and Jessica. I'll be back in a minute."

With that she hurried acorss the crowded cafeteria, her heart hammering with excitement. *I'm not finished yet*, she thought jubilantly.

There was still time to get Tom assigned to Jean. And not even Jean West was going to be able to pull this one off!

"I don't know, Sandy," Lila said, frowning down at her pad of paper. "We really want Jeanie to get in. Don't you think Tom McKay's kind of a risk?"

Sandra took a deep breath. The sorority meeting was about to begin, and she had only a minute or two left to convince Lila that Tom was a good candidate for Jean's first pledge task.

"Come on," she said lightly. "Tom will jump at the chance to go out with Jeanie. Any guy would!"

"Well, I agree with you about 'any guy,' " Lila said, wrinkling her brow. "But Tom? I just don't think it's a very good idea."

Tom McKay was one of the best-looking boys in the junior class. Blond and clean-cut, he was on the tennis team. He was also a whiz at science and loved any kind of outdoor activity, biking, camping, boating. He was exactly the kind of guy most girls dreamed about, but he seldom dated. The last girl he'd gone with was Jessica Wakefield, and a few people joked that she had turned him off the female sex forever, having strung him along until someone better came along.

Of all the guys Sandra could think of, Tom McKay was the least likely to be interested in Jean. For all her skill at sports, Jean wasn't an outdoorsy sort of girl. She loved dressing up and going dancing or seeing a movie and getting something to eat. And she liked slick, sophisticated guys, not the rugged, outdoor sort.

And if Jean had snubbed Tom in some way, Sandra knew Tom well enough to suspect he wouldn't be big on the idea of giving her a second chance. He was easily hurt, and apparently Jean had hurt him.

But Sandra didn't say any of this to Lila. What she said was that Jean would be able to wrap Tom around her little finger in seconds. "Besides," she added, chuckling, "Jeanie loves a challenge."

"Well," Lila said, "you know her better than I do. If you say so—"

"She'll get him to say yes. Don't worry," Sandra said cheerfully.

"OK, we've got to get started," Lila said, turning to the crowd of sorority members who had filed into the lounge. "This is just going to take a couple of minutes, and I only need sponsors to stay. The rest of you can go. I just wanted to let you know that our first pledge party will be this Saturday night at Cara's apartment. The pledges will be assigned dates, and their first pledge task is to make sure their dates come—and stay." Everyone laughed.

Sandra listened with immense relief as Lila read off the list of pledges and their assigned "dates." Everything was going to be all right after all, she thought happily.

She knew Jean would be a little disappointed about Pi Beta, but she was sure it would wear off. As long as Jean never found out Sandra was the one who kept her from getting in . . .

Sandra didn't feel guilty anymore about her plan. She was convinced it was the only way to preserve her friendship with Jean. Strange as it seemed, she had to do something hurtful to make sure Jean wouldn't just forget her. Yes, she *had* to keep Jean out of Pi Beta. With Tom McKay's help, she might just be able to do it.

Three

"Sandy!" Jean wailed, looking absolutely miserable. "I can't even get Tom McKay to say *hello* to me, let alone come as my date to Cara's party!"

Sandra pretended to look surprised. "Why? I always thought Tom was really sweet. Don't you know him?"

Jean shook her head, looking distressed. "He's—I don't know. He's just really hard to talk to. Couldn't you have chosen someone a little easier for me?"

Sandra thought fast. The girls were sitting together on the grass in front of school, enjoying a few minutes of sun before the lunch hour ended. Sandra could see Lila in the distance, and she wasn't sure how much longer she'd have to talk to Jean alone. "Listen, Jeanie," she said, dropping her voice confidentially, "I'm a little afraid some of the other girls think I'm playing favorites with you as it is. I don't want them to think I'm trying to make the pledge period easy for you. It could get you in trouble if I did."

Jean's eyes widened. "You think of everything, Sandy," she said gratefully. "You know, that never even occurred to me. Does anyone really think you're trying to give me special treatment?"

Sandra looked thoughtful. "No one's said anything, but I've definitely been getting strange vibes. But promise not to say a word. I could be completely wrong."

"Still," Jean said, watching Lila approach, "you're absolutely right to take precautions, Sandy. I don't want anything to mess up my chances of getting in!"

"Hey, you two!" Lila called. A minute later she plopped down beside them on the grass and began fanning herself with her notebook. I'm telling you, trying to organize pledge season is going to be the end of me."

"You're not the only one." Jean giggled. "Lila, have you got any advice on how to tame Tom McKay? I'm convinced he hates me," she added reflectively. "He started talking to me about something just yesterday, and I was in the middle of doing something and couldn't answer. He looked like he was ready to kill me!"

"Hmmm," Lila said. "Maybe he's just shy."

"I don't think so," Jean said, sighing. "I think he really hates me."

"I know what!" Lila cried, snapping her fingers. "I probably shouldn't be helping you," she added, looking around warily, "but since you *do* have kind of a tough assignment, I don't see anything really wrong with dropping a hint or two."

"Come on," Jean begged. "I need all the help I can get."

"Well," Lila said, her dark eyes twinkling, "I happen to know Tom's only playing in the first part of the match this afternoon. He's playing doubles with Bruce Patman, but his singles match has been canceled because the guy from Orion High is sick."

Jean looked a bit discouraged. "I'm not sure I get it, Lila. Am I being really stupid?"

"Well, let's say the three of us just *happen* to go watch the match," Lila said coyly. "When Tom finishes, you can sort of casually tell him how well he played and how much you *adore* tennis and how you've always wished you could get to know him a little better, but he's always in such a *hurry*—"

"I get it now," Jean said. "Though I'm not sure it'll work half as well when *I* try it."

"Oh, I think you'll do just fine. Don't you think so, Sandy?" Lila asked.

Sandra forced a smile. "You'll do great," she mumbled. She wished Lila hadn't come over to sit with them. Just when everything seemed to be going so well . . .

All she could do now was hope Jean and Lila's scheme backfired. Once Tom agreed to go to Cara's party, Jean would be as good as pledged to Pi Beta Alpha.

"Cara, what's with you today? You're not even listening to me!" Jessica complained.

"Sorry, Jess," she muttered. "What did you say?"

"I *said*, if there's anything I can do to help you out on Saturday night, just let me know."

Cara smiled. "You're sweet to volunteer, Jess. And I may take you up on it."

"You don't sound very excited," Jessica observed. "Are you sorry we're not having Steve's party at your place?"

Cara shook her head, her eyes lowered. "No . . ." she said slowly.

"Well, what *is* it, then?"

Cara reddened slightly. "Everything *isn't* OK," she admitted finally.

Jessica looked triumphant. "Now we're getting somewhere!" she exclaimed. "Well?" she added. "Aren't you going to at least give me a hint?"

Cara's eyes filled with tears. "I don't want to talk about it."

Jessica stared at her. She knew Cara had been through some difficult months following her parents' separation and divorce and her father's moving away. But she thought that was all in the past now. Since she had started seeing Steven, Cara had been much happier—more like her old self, but with a new sensitivity.

"It isn't anything to do with Steve, is it?" Jessica asked. To her surprise, Cara burst into tears.

"Y-yes," she said at last. "It is."

"Is it another woman?" Jessica asked sympathetically.

Cara shook her head. "I don't think so," she said. "I'm pretty sure he isn't interested in anyone but me."

Jessica stared at her. "Then what's the trouble?" she demanded. The next minute her aqua eyes widened in horror. "You're not going to break his heart, are you? Have *you* met someone else?"

Cara laughed, despite the tears still clinging to her dark lashes. "You're amazing, Jess. Hasn't it ever occurred to you that something *else* could go wrong?"

"If you'd quit making me play guessing games, maybe I'd be enlightened," Jessica said. "Come on, Cara. What's up?"

Cara sighed. "Jess, I really want to talk to you about it. But you're his sister, and he made me promise not to tell you."

Jessica paled. "Is something wrong with him? Is he in some kind of trouble?"

Cara sighed. "Well, yes and no. I guess I'd better tell you—but, Jessica Wakefield, you have to swear not to tell Liz or your parents. Do you swear?"

"I swear," Jessica said promptly.

"Well," Cara said, looking unhappy, "apparently Steve's roommate Bob's father owns an ocean liner, one of those ships used just for cruises. Every few months the ship goes from L.A. to the Far East and then on to Europe. Anyway, Bob's decided to leave school to work for his dad, and he's convinced Steve to quit college and go along!"

"Wow," Jessica said, her eyes shining. "I think it sounds great, Cara. Ocean liners are so romantic. Maybe you can stow away and creep out on the upper deck when you're smack in the middle of the ocean, like on 'Love Boat,' "

Cara looked annoyed. "Jess, this isn't TV. And I can't stow away! If Steve goes, I'll never see him again."

28

"I see your point," Jessica said. "Boy, my parents aren't going to be one bit happy if Steve drops out of college. Does he seem like he's got his mind made up?"

Cara nodded, fresh tears welling up in her eyes. "What am I going to do?" she wailed.

Jessica shook her head. "I don't know," she said. She wished she hadn't promised to keep this quiet.

She was going to go crazy until Steven came home on Friday and told everyone himself!

"I can't believe how long it takes to play one lousy game of doubles," Jean grumbled. "I hope this works, you guys. Otherwise, we've all wasted a perfectly beautiful afternoon."

"Shh," Lila warned. "They're done, Jeanie. Now we've just got to corner Tom."

Sandra looked in the other direction, willing Tom to ignore Lila and Jean with all her might. To her dismay, he looked up wth a smile when Lila called his name. "Come keep us company," Lila sang out, patting the bench beside her.

"I don't know," Tom said, shielding his eyes with his hand and squinting up at them. "I should probably sit with the team. Coach says—"

"Please, Tom," Jean purred, flashing him her most winning smile. "You played so well," she added. "Only I don't really understand the finer points. Why don't you just sit with me and tell me a little about what's really going on. It would all be so much more fun that way."

To Sandra's disbelief, Tom seemed to be thinking it over. "All right," he said finally. "Let me just tell the coach so he won't think I've defected."

A few minutes later he bounded up the bleachers and sat next to Jean. A white towel hung casually around his neck. Sandra couldn't get over it. Granted, he seemed somewhat confused by Jean's friendliness. But little by little he warmed up, and by the time the first set was over, he, Jean, and Lila were joking and laughing like old friends.

"I have to admit I'm kind of surprised to see you three here," he said sometime later. "Lila, I know you're a pro, but I didn't think you two were interested in tennis." He looked at Jean and Sandra as he said this.

"Jeanie is," Lila said promptly. "She's been dying to take lessons. Haven't you, Jeanie?"

Blushing, Jean stared at her. "Uh—yes, as a matter of fact, I have," she mumbled.

Tom looked delighted. "Maybe I could give you a few pointers," he volunteered. "I've never actually given lessons, but I'm working at the Tennis Shop now, and I've taken enough lessons to have a pretty good idea how to teach a beginner."

"I'd love that," Jean said shyly. Lila poked Sandra in the ribs with her elbow. "What about this weekend?" Jean added, getting bolder.

Tom frowned. "Well, I work at the store all day Saturday. And Sunday isn't so good for me. But maybe . . ." He thought fast and seemed to reach a conclusion. "My parents have a flood-lit court, so we could play Saturday night. Are you free then?"

Jean shifted awkwardly on the hard bench. She knew this was her opportunity, but she felt bad somehow, having set up Tom this way and tricking him in front of Lila and Sandra. Still, a pledge task was a pledge task. If all the other girls had to do it . . .

She took a deep breath. "As a matter of fact, I *am* busy this Saturday night," she said regretfully. "Cara Walker's having a party. Hey," she said, trying to make it sound as if the idea had just occurred to her, "if you're not doing anything, how would you like to come to Cara's with me?"

Tom looked astounded. "With *you*?" he repeated blankly.

Jean nodded. "I mean, if you're not doing anything. I just thought—"

"Well," Tom said, smiling, "that doesn't do

much to settle your tennis troubles, but sure, I'd like to come along. Why don't I give you a call later in the week and find out when it starts and everything?''

Sandra looked away again as Jean and Tom exchanged telephone numbers. No doubt about it—her first scheme had backfired.

Now she was going to have to come up with some way to make sure Tom ditched Jean at the last minute. Come to think of it, if Tom stood Jean up, she'd look even worse than if he had turned her down.

And it couldn't be *that* hard to convince Tom that Jean was just using him. Actually, Sandra thought, all she really had to do was tell him the truth.

Four

"You know, I've got the weirdest feeling about the Pi Beta pledge period," Jean said dreamily. She was curled up on the couch in the Wests' living room, barely paying attention to the video she and Sandra had rented to watch that night.

"What do you mean?" Sandra asked uneasily.

Jean shrugged, flipping her silky hair off her shoulder. "It's hard to explain. You'll think I'm being silly if I tell you."

Frowning, Sandra sat up straighter, "I will not," she protested. "Come on, Jeanie. What do you mean?"

It was Friday evening, and the girls were dressed in bright-colored sweats, ready for one of their long, comfortable evenings in front of the TV set, gossiping about the events of the week behind them and the weekend to come.

But Sandra just couldn't relax. All she could think about was the pledge party the next night at Cara's. Jean's anticipation was so vivid, and Sandra couldn't help feeling guilty. Friends were meant to share each other's happiness, not to get in happiness's way! she reminded herself. But Pi Beta was the only thing Sandra felt she had that was hers exclusively. Once Jean had that, too, she wouldn't need Sandra anymore. That was what was killing Sandra, what was making her feel prepared to go to any lengths to stop Jean from making it through the pledge period.

"What I mean is this," Jean said, her green eyes shining with intensity. "It's like some kind of lucky spell's been put on me. I know that sounds ridiculous, but it's true." She giggled. "Penny Ayala is on the dance committee for the Friday the Thirteenth dance a week from tonight, and she asked Dana Larson and me to start off the dancing because we both have birthdays that day. That's supposed to be unlucky, isn't it?" She giggled again. "But ever since you nominated me for Pi Beta, I've never felt so lucky."

"What do you mean?" Sandra asked again, staring at her.

"Well, for one thing, my father told me a few days ago that a bond my grandparents bought for me years ago has matured, and he gave me a hundred dollars, just out of the blue! So I'm going to buy something special to wear tomorrow night. Then," she continued, "I got an A on my history exam. You know how busy I've been with cheerleading and everything. I didn't even have time to study. But the essay question was on the only thing I knew about, the Civil War."

Sandra took a sip of her diet soda. "You're *always* lucky, Jeanie," she said gloomily.

Jean shook her head. "Well, that's not all," she said. "The luckiest thing has been getting stuck with Tom McKay for tomorrow night. Do you realize we actually had a decent talk when he called me? He's really nice, too."

Sandra pushed her soda away in disgust. "So he's looking forward to Cara's party, huh?"

Jean nodded. "Apparently! And you know something, Sandy, so am I. To be honest with you, I wasn't exactly big on the idea of Tom when you told me he was my assignment. But he's really OK." Her eyes twinkled. "Who knows? I might really start to like him!"

Sandra sighed heavily. This was even worse than she had expected. How was she going to convince Tom to ditch Jean if he was counting the minutes until Cara's party?

"He even wants to go out to get something to

eat first," Jean confided. "He's going to pick me up early because the party starts at eight-thirty, right?"

Sandra nodded. She was only listening with half an ear. The last thing she had expected was that Tom McKay and Jean would actually *like* each other!

"Isn't he really obsessed with sports, though?" Sandra objected. "I thought you hated jocks."

As Jean tucked her legs up underneath her, a little smile played about her lips. "I don't know," she murmured. "Maybe I was a little hasty, Sandy. All I know is that I'm not dreading tomorrow night half as much as I thought I would be!"

Well, there goes that, Sandra thought. Unless she did something drastic, it looked as if Tom was going to do exactly what Jean wanted him to do the following night.

Sandra felt terrible. She just couldn't let it happen! If doing something drastic was the only way to keep Jean out of Pi Beta Alpha, then Sandra was prepared to do something drastic.

It looked as though her only option was to find Tom the next day and drop a couple of significant hints about Cara's party.

Maybe if he realized his dream date was only using him, he'd be a little less excited about being her escort!

*   *   *

"Steve, do you have any idea how good it is to have you home again?" Elizabeth asked.

Steven leaned over to rumple her hair, his dark eyes twinkling. "It isn't half bad being home, either," he said. "Especially around dinner time! I'm telling you, that dorm food makes a hunger strike sound appealing."

The Wakefields were sitting out on the patio in the twilight, eating barbecued chicken and asking Steven questions about college life. Jessica was the only one who was quiet. Taking a mouthful of salad, she sneaked a look at her brother, wondering when he was planning to spill the big news. She couldn't help thinking how good Steven looked. Broad-shouldered and dark-haired, he had the kind of casual good looks that made people naturally gravitate to him. With his pleasant manners and excellent sense of humor, he had always been popular. He would be a natural on an ocean liner, Jessica thought suddenly. She couldn't believe she had been skeptical before. All the same, she knew her parents were going to be upset about his decision.

But Jessica was not prepared for how upset her parents were when Steven broached the subject of leaving college.

"Steve, you're not serious," Mrs. Wakefield

said, her blue eyes narrowing with concern. "You're only a freshman. You've barely given college a chance!"

"Mom, I'm sick of studying," Steven said earnestly. "I don't mind school, but I feel I want something more—experience, a chance to see the world! I've been in school all my life," he complained. "I really feel ready to leave and get a job."

Mr. Wakefield frowned. "You know, Steve, the way things are today, it's harder and harder to get a job without special training of one kind or another. Don't you think leaving college now would jeopardize your chances of finding a good job?"

Steven shook his head. "That's the great thing. I've already got a job all lined up!"

Mr. and Mrs. Wakefield exchanged worried glances. "What kind of job?" Mrs. Wakefield asked.

"You know my roommate, Bob, right? Well, his father owns an ocean liner called the *Bellefleur*. You guys should see it. It's the most beautiful ship in the whole world. He runs cruises from Los Angeles to the Far East and then on around the world. Bob says I can get a job on the ship!"

"I don't want to dispel your enthusiasm,"

Mr. Wakefield said dryly, "but exactly what sort of job would it be?"

Steven shrugged. "I don't know. Maybe being a bartender, maybe a waiter. Nothing fancy, but an opportunity like this comes along once in a lifetime. I'd get to see the whole world!"

Mr. Wakefield smiled. "That reminds me of a joke I heard the other day. One guy says, 'My daughter went around the world this summer.' And the other guy says, 'Oh, really? Where's she going next summer?'"

Mrs. Wakefield sighed. "Ned, this isn't exactly a joking matter. I think Steve's serious about this."

"Of course I'm serious," Steven broke in. "I've already talked to my adviser at school. I'll go back to school next week. The following week I'll sign the contract with Mr. Rose. He's out of town right now. Then I'll pack up my things and sail a few days after that!"

"What about Cara?" Elizabeth asked, obviously shocked by her brother's announcement.

Steven frowned. "She's having a hard time accepting it," he admitted. "But I'm hoping I can talk to her about it and help her understand that it's really the best thing for me right now. It'll be hard, being separated, but—"

"Steven," Mr. Wakefield said sternly, "I think you, your mother, and I need to discuss this

39

alone. This isn't the sort of thing you rush into, you understand. Nobody's getting on any ocean liner before we've all had some very serious discussions."

Steven got to his feet. "I do understand, Dad," he said softly. "But my mind is made up. This is *my* life, not yours or Mom's. And no one's going to stop me from sailing on the *Bellefleur*. No one."

The next minute he had crossed the patio and entered the house, closing the sliding glass door quietly but firmly behind him.

"What are we going to do?" Mrs. Wakefield cried, distraught.

Mr. Wakefield frowned. "It may just be a phase," he said, not sounding very hopeful. "Or maybe something's wrong at school. If we can talk to him . . ."

"I think it's an excellent idea," Jessica protested. "Why shouldn't he sail around the world? I wouldn't mind going, myself."

Mrs. Wakefield glared at her. "Jess, try to be a little sensitive, OK? This isn't a joking matter."

"Mom," Elizabeth said, a thoughtful expression on her face, "remember when you got that job offer in San Francisco and Jessica and I ambushed you and Daddy with propaganda about Sweet Valley, trying to convince you to stay?"

Mrs. Wakefield looked perplexed. "Of course I do, honey." She smiled. "You two were pretty darn persuasive, too, though that wasn't the reason I didn't take the job."

"Listen," Elizabeth said earnestly, "maybe we should try a little bit of the same medicine on Steve—only let's try a little reverse psychology this time."

"What do you mean?" Mr. Wakefield asked, looking skeptical.

"Jess is the one who gave me the idea." Elizabeth said, sounding excited. "Her response is exactly the right line to take. Instead of getting all upset about Steve's decision, maybe we should all act like it's no big deal. Let's approve of it one hundred percent. In fact," she added with a giggle, "the surprise party we've been planning for a week from tomorrow can be a bon voyage party instead. If he thinks we're all behind him . . ."

Jessica's face lit up. "Liz is right," she said enthusiastically. "He probably came home expecting everyone to throw a fit. Instead, we should all encourage him to go! Mom, you can take him shopping for luggage. I'll talk to Cara and convince her to act like she couldn't care less if he goes."

Mr. Wakefield began to smile. "The kids just might be right, Alice," he admitted. "Steve may

41

be feeling as though he needs to prove he's old enough to do what he wants. If we don't put up any opposition, the idea of dropping out of school may lose its appeal."

Mrs. Wakefield looked worried. "I don't know," she said anxiously. "What if he goes ahead and does it anyway? Then all we'll have done is make his departure easier."

Elizabeth shook her head. "Trust us, Mom," she said. "As long as we *all* go along with it and no one says a single negative thing about his plans, I guarantee Steve will change his mind faster than you can say 'drop out'!"

"Well," Mrs. Wakefield said at last, "I guess it's worth a try."

Elizabeth jumped to her feet.

"Where are you going?" Jessica demanded.

Elizabeth grinned. "Oh, just upstairs," she said casually. "I want to see if Steve needs help packing, and if he wants to borrow my camera while he's away!"

Jessica giggled, catching on. "I'd better see if he wants me to buy him some airmail stationery. He's going to need it, since that's the only way he'll be able to keep in touch with anyone from the middle of the Pacific."

The next minute the twins were hurrying inside. Elizabeth couldn't wait to put their scheme into action. She was almost positive Steven wouldn't want to go once he had faced the implications of dropping out of college and leaving home.

The only question was whether or not the Wakefields could make him change his mind in the one week he was spending at home before going back to Mr. Rose to sign the contract.

Five

Sandra parked her mother's Toyota in front
of the Valley Mall entrance, then checked her
reflection in the rearview mirror. Sandra was so
nervous her heart was pounding. She had never
done anything like this before. Two-thirty, the
digital clock on the dashboard said. Tom ought
to be through with lunch by now, and with any
luck the Tennis Shop would be fairly empty. It
was such a beautiful afternoon, too beautiful to
be inside.

Ten minutes later Sandra was pretending to
inspect a frilly tennis dress inside the store. The
shop was divided into two parts. The front half
of the store was filled with clothes racks crammed
with tennis clothes of every color and style.
Tennis shoes lined one wall. The back of the
store was where tennis rackets and balls were

sold. Dropping the price tag on the dress, Sandra caught sight of Tom emerging from the storeroom, his arms laden with rackets. Pretending she hadn't seen him, Sandra moved over to look at shoes.

"Can I help you, miss?" Tom said behind her.

Sandra turned around, her eyebrows shooting up with feigned surprise. "Tom! I completely forgot you worked here."

Tom smiled. "I didn't know you were a tennis fan, Sandy. Are you looking for a pair of shoes?"

"They're for my mother, actually," Sandra lied, picking up the nearest pair. "Can I see these in a size seven?"

"Sure," Tom said. A few minutes later he emerged from the back room and took the tennis shoes out of their box. "You think these will do?"

Sandra looked at the shoes, wiping her palms on her shorts. How could she change the subject from tennis shoes? She was so bad at this sort of thing! "I wish I could play," she said lamely, "but I'm so busy—between cheerleading and Pi Beta Alpha . . ."

Tom looked interested. "Jean mentioned she wanted to get into Pi Beta," he said. "Is it a big deal?"

Sandra thought fast. "Well, yes and no," she said, fiddling with the lace on one of the shoes. "Pledging can be pretty grueling for some girls. They have to do all sorts of tasks. You know," she added, trying to sound casual, "sometimes it's even things like getting a guy to be your date who seems impossible. Or wearing a silly outfit to school—something like that."

Tom stared at her, an uneasy expression crossing his face. "How long does the pledge period last?"

"Well, part of it ends tonight," Sandra said. She tried to make her face look slightly upset and surprised, as if she'd just remembered something. "*You're* coming to Cara's party, aren't you?"

Tom frowned. "You mean tonight's party has something to do with the sorority? It isn't part of the pledging thing, is it?"

This time Sandra's embarrassed stare was natural. "Uh . . . yes and no," she said miserably.

Tom's eyes flashed with anger. "Do you mean to tell me—"

"Tom, I've got to get going," Sandra said quickly, grabbing her handbag and hurrying away.

"What about the shoes?" he called after her. But Sandra didn't turn around. She couldn't believe what she had just done. Her eyes were filled with guilty tears, and she could barely find her way out of the store and into the mall.

I just hope Jean doesn't find out, she thought miserably. *If Tom confronts her and she finds out I was the one who ratted on her, she'll never talk to me again as long as she lives!*

Tom put the last racket cover away. He had finished doing inventory, and he knew he could go home now. But he didn't feel like it. He was burning mad, and he was afraid once he went home, he'd do nothing but sit and stew over what Sandra had accidentally blurted out.

So Jean was just using him as a pledge task. It was painfully obvious when he put the bits and pieces of Sandra's story together. The pledges were given various assignments, and sometimes one assignment was to get a particular guy to go out.

Boy, he'd sure fallen for it that time. *What an idiot I am*, he thought miserably. For ages he had had a secret crush on Jean West. Who wouldn't? She was petite, slender, and pretty, with long, gleaming dark brown hair and eyes as green as meadow grass. Jean West's middle name could have been Perfect, but that had always been part of the trouble.

Tom was shy around girls. Maybe not outwardly shy—after all, he had managed to date

Jessica Wakefield, one of the most popular and flirtatious girls at school. But when it came to making a commitment, to really caring, *then* he was shy. The truth was, he had never been in love. Jean was the first girl whom he had been interested in in a long time.

But he didn't like the way Jean acted sometimes. Granted, she was pretty. But Tom had never been sure there was anything beyond Jean's image. The few times he had tried to strike up a conversation with her, she had seemed aloof. When she did respond, she didn't really seem to have much to say; she just made small talk.

Gradually Tom's interest in Jean had faded. He had been astounded when she had approached him at the tennis match. And Tom was extremely flattered. Not only had she and Lila called him over, but Jean had gone all out trying to talk to him. And she didn't just chatter that time—she really *talked*. They had had some great telephone conversations, too, and Tom felt as if he was beginning to like her. He had been looking forward to their date so much. He had even bought a new shirt and had gotten permission to take his father's car. . . .

Well, I was a jerk, he thought sharply. *A real jerk. I'm not going to let her make a fool of me in front of everyone tonight.*

He couldn't believe Jean would do this to him. But from what Sandra had let slip, there was no denying it. It was too much of a coincidence. Here this gorgeous girl had approached him out of the blue and asked him to a party that just happened to be one of the most important events in the Pi Beta Alpha pledge period!

Well, I'll show her, Tom thought grimly.

He had no intention of letting Jean know that he knew what she was up to. Better fo fight fire with fire, he decided. Let her go on thinking everything was perfectly fine—until it was too late for her to do anything about it.

There was no way he was going to be her date that night. He was going to make her good and sorry she had treated him the way she had. And he was going to make *her* look like a fool in front of her sorority sisters!

"Who is it?" Steven called.

"Only me," Elizabeth said, opening the door to his bedroom a crack and sticking her head inside. "Can I come in?"

"Sure," Steven said.

Elizabeth strolled into her brother's bedroom and plopped down in his armchair, watching Steven search through some papers on his desk. "I was just thinking," she said conversationally, "that you probably won't be wanting your word processor on board the *Bellefleur*, right?"

Steven stared at her. "I get the definite impression you're hinting, Liz."

Elizabeth smiled. "Well, I have an awful lot of stuff to do for *The Oracle* these days, Steve. A computer of my own would sure come in handy. And if you're not going to be using yours anymore . . ."

Steven stiffened. "I worked hard to buy that computer, Liz."

"I'll take excellent care of it," Elizabeth said. "Come on, Steve. What are you going to do with a computer in the middle of the ocean?"

Steven didn't say anything at first. "I'll think about it," he said shortly, turning back to the papers on his desk.

"What's that?" Elizabeth asked him, trying hard to keep her voice nonchalant.

Steven made a face. "A bunch of junk Dad gave me this morning, insurance policies, medical plans, all that sort of thing. He says I'll have to check out my coverage now that I'm leaving school." He frowned again. "I never realized how much paperwork it takes just to stay healthy."

Elizabeth smiled. Poor Steven was getting the treatment, all right. He didn't seem to know how to react to his family's sudden decision to let him do whatever he wanted—and even to back him in his plans. "Liz," he said now, looking earnest, "I'm glad Mom and Dad see this thing my way and are going to let me go."

"Well, as you said last night, Steve, you're really old enough to do what you think is best. I think Mom and Dad may have been a little disappointed at first, but you've convinced them that this really is the opportunity of a lifetime. Why *wouldn't* they support you?"

"Well," Steven said, swallowing, "it really is a great opportunity, you know. Except I'll hardly ever see any of you guys. I'll be gone for eight or nine months at a time.

"Oh, eight or nine months is nothing," Elizabeth scoffed. "We can always write each other letters! And think how exciting it'll be. You'll get to see the Far East, and Europe—all kinds of exotic places."

"Of course," Steven said thoughtfully, "there's my future to consider. I guess I'm kind of surprised Mom and Dad caved in so easily."

Aha! Elizabeth thought. It was working already! And once Cara got to him that night. . . . Elizabeth could have wept for Steven, he looked so confused. But she reminded herself the plan would work only if they all kept it up. "Well, I think you convinced them that this is what you really want," Elizabeth said earnestly. "I mean, not everyone wants a college education, Steve. For some people it's just the wrong thing. If you really feel you're wasting your time—"

Steven stood up abruptly. "It isn't really that I feel I'm wasting my time, Liz. I just feel I want to get started, you know? Like so much of my life so far has been preparing me for the next step. Now I'm eighteen, and I don't know. I just want things to happen!"

Elizabeth was quiet for a minute. "Well, that's why I think you're doing the right thing," she said at last. "You know what Daddy always says about short-term and long-term goals. It sounds as if your goals are pretty much all directed toward *right now*. So what's the point in going through all that school?"

Steven paced around his bedroom, deep in thought. "Cara won't understand at all," he said at last. "She's been completely hysterical about it. She acts as if we'll never see each other again."

"Well, you can't blame Cara if she decides she can't wait eight or nine months to see you each time," Elizabeth said reasonably. "Look, Steve, every decision has advantages and disadvantages. I think you're excited enough about this new job and all the places you'll see to offset a little thing like missing Cara."

Steven didn't respond to this. "I haven't seen

her yet," he mused aloud. "I'll bet she flips at her party tonight and starts begging me not to go, the way she did on the phone last week."

Elizabeth smiled to herself. Jessica had been on the phone with Cara for almost an hour that morning, and from the report Elizabeth had heard, there wasn't much chance of Cara's making a scene.

Cara thought the Wakefields' plan was a great idea, and she was all set to act as though Steven's decision were absolutely fine with her. In fact, she was going to add an extra little twist, Jessica said, though Cara wouldn't tell her what it was.

Elizabeth had a feeling that it was going to be some party!

Six

Jean looked anxiously at herself in the full-length mirror in her walk-in closet. She wished someone were at home to tell her if she looked all right, but her parents and all her brothers had left almost an hour earlier for a movie downtown. She thought the new narrow skirt, over-size shirt and soft leather hip belt suited her, and she knew her hair was behaving itself. It was even shinier than usual, and the kohl pencil under her eyes looked pretty sexy.

Who would ever have guessed she would be looking forward to an evening with Tom McKay this much? It wasn't that Tom wasn't cute. It was just that she wasn't very experienced and still tended to make snap judgments about boys. She had decided ages ago that she had had it with most guys. Growing up in a household of brothers, there had been endless talk about sports and camping trips. She wanted to meet a sophisticated, urbane guy, maybe a little older, who knew about theater and music. Someone she could really talk to.

Tom hadn't impressed her as that kind of guy. He was much more like her brothers—good-natured, frank, down to earth—the sort of guy she would never have really paid attention to if she hadn't been assigned to him by the Pi Betas.

All the same, she had enjoyed every conversation they'd had, and she found herself thinking about him a great deal. He really *was* good looking. Maybe he didn't know that much about theater, but to be honest, neither did she. She found Tom refreshing and easy to be with. It was like being with a friend, only with—her heart beat a little faster, thinking about his broad shoulders and crooked smile—something *more*.

She dabbed a little of her best perfume on her wrists and throat, wondering what that evening was going to be like. She wondered if there would be dancing at Cara's. She wondered what it would feel like to have Tom's arms around her. She stared at her face in the mirror, feeling her cheeks going hot. Would he kiss her? Would he—?

The chime in the clock downstairs sounded, and Jean paused to count. It was seven-thirty already. Tom should be there any minute now! He had said he'd come by in plenty of time to get something to eat before the party. Jean put on earrings and applied on a little more makeup. To her surprise, the minutes went on, and there was no sign of Tom. *That's funny*, she thought. *He made a point of calling to see if I could be ready early. And now he's half an hour late.*

By eight-fifteen Jean was beginning to worry. "Maybe I should call him," she said aloud, pacing back and forth downstairs with her jacket in her arms. She didn't want to make him think she was overeager, but the truth was, she was starving. And she didn't want to be late to Cara's. That night was a big part of the pledge period, and she wanted everything to go perfectly.

Pi Beta Alpha meant even more to her now than it had a few weeks before. She had always thought it would be fun to belong, but lately her desire to get in had multiplied. She was convinced it would allow her to spend more time with Sandra and make them even closer than they were. Lately Sandra had been acting strange. Jean felt they were beginning to drift apart, and the thought of losing her friend made her feel terrible. She hoped joining the sorority would help close the gap between them. Sandra's friendship meant more to her than anything in the world. If something were to happen to jeopardize that friendship . . .

Jean was deep in thought when the telephone rang. She hurried to the phone, glancing at her watch as she did so. It was twenty minutes to nine.

"Jeanie? It's Tom," a familiar voice said.

"Tom, where *are* you?" Jean shrieked. "I've been really worried."

Tom cleared his throat. "I'm sorry," he said, sounding rueful, "but I wasn't feeling well when I got back from work, so I lay down for a few minutes and just woke up. I'll be over in a couple of minutes. I guess you'd better grab a sandwich or something, Jeanie. I'm really sorry."

"That's all right," Jean said. As long as you're OK, I don't mind. See you soon, then."

"See you soon," Tom agreed, hanging up the phone.

Jean made herself a sandwich, her eyes on the clock. She was definitely going to be late to Cara's. Was Tom playing games with her, or had he been telling the truth?

On an impulse she dialed Cara's number. It was nine o'clock and the party was apparently in full swing. It was almost impossible to hear Cara's voice over the pulsating music in the background.

"Jeanie, where are you?" Cara asked. "We've all been waiting for you!"

"Tom's late. He says he'll be here any minute," Jean said apologetically. "Tell everyone I'm really sorry, OK?"

"He isn't standing you up, is he?" Cara said, then laughed.

Jean bit her lip. She didn't think that was anything to joke about. She had been wondering the same thing herself.

By nine-thirty Jean was beginning to panic. They were going to be embarrassingly late, even if Tom *did* show up. What could he possibly have been doing all this time? Her face burned every time she imagined having to explain this to Lila, Cara, Jessica, and the other Pi Betas. Sandra, of course, would understand, but everyone else would think she was the biggest loser who ever lived.

At quarter to ten the phone rang again. "Jeanie, I feel terrible," Tom croaked into the phone.

"You *sound* terrible," Jean said glumly. "Tom, where are you? What's going on?"

"I think I have food poisoning. I'm in Fowler Memorial Hospital, in the emergency room. I tried to drive over to your place, but I couldn't make it. I felt like I was going to pass out, and I kept getting sick."

59

Jean's brow wrinkled. "You really must be sick!" she exclaimed. "You're honestly in the hospital?"

Tom sighed. "Yes, and I'm afraid I'll be here for a few hours. They think they may have to pump my stomach. I guess I ate something bad at lunch."

"You poor thing," Jean said sympathetically. "Do you want me to come over and keep you company?"

Tom paused. "No," he said. "Go ahead. Go to Cara's. I'm sure I'll be fine."

Jean thought it over quickly. "Well, I'll call you tomorrow morning, then, to see how you feel. OK?"

Tom didn't answer, and apparently they got disconnected because Jean heard a click and then a dial tone. *Oh, well*, she thought philosophically. *If he's sick, he's sick.* At least she had a good excuse for being late!

"Jeanie, Jeanie, Jeanie," Lila said, shaking her head. "You're the *last* person we would have expected to show up without a date tonight. All the other girls managed to drag *their* assignments here!"

Jean felt terrible. She could see the crowd in the living room, talking and dancing to the music playing on the stereo. Amy Sutton was danc-

ag dreamily in the arms of Aaron Dallas, her
ssigned date. All the other pledges had managed
> make things the way they should. All but Jean.

"Tom was planning to come, but he got food
oisoning," Jean defended herself. "Wasn't he,
andy?" she asked, turning to Sandra with an
mploring look on her face.

Sandra looked away. "I guess we really ought
> check out Jeanie's story," she said at last. "I
nean, this *is* one of the biggest tests in the
ledge season, and Jeanie's the only one who
asn't succeeded."

Jean reddened to the roots of her hair. She
>uldn't believe Sandra was the one pointing
nat out!

Lila and Jessica looked surprised, too. "I'm
ure Jeanie's telling the truth," Lila said, staring
t Sandra.

"But," Sandra said calmly, "Tom might not
e."

"OK," Jean said quickly. "What should I do?
'ou want me to call the hospital?"

There was a brief pause, and then Lila said,
)oking hesitant, "Well, maybe you should, if
ou don't mind, Jeanie."

Still blushing furiously, Jean called directory
ssistance, got the hospital's number, and then
alled the emergency room.

"I'm sorry," the nurse said. "No one by tha name has been here this evening. Did you sa McKale?"

"McKay," Jean repeated. This, she decidec was the most humiliating thing that had eve happened to her.

"No, " the nurse said. "No McKale *or* McKay.

Jean hung the phone up and turned slowly t face the others. "Well," she said, ready to burs into tears, "Sandra's right. He was lying. H isn't there."

No one said anything for a minute, and Jea felt her tears spill over. "Does that mean I can get into Pi Beta Alpha?" she blurted out.

Lila put her arm around her. "Poor thing, she said. "That guy must be a total idiot, stand ing you up. He doesn't know his head from hole in the ground!"

"Pledge period isn't over yet," Cara chime in. "Maybe we can figure out some way for yo to do something else to make up for tonight Something easy," she added, smiling fondly a Jean as she handed her a tissue.

Jean took it gratefully. "I've got an idea," sh said, her eyes beginning to shine. "I think I'v got a plan that just *may* make Mr. McKay sorr he pulled this little trick on me tonight."

"What is it?" Jessica asked, intrigued.

"Let's say I act as though I believed hin

tonight. As though I really like him and want to get to know him better," Jean said. "I'll get my hooks into him this week and make sure he starts to care about me. And *then* I'll ask him to be my date at the dance on Friday. Remember, Dana and I are supposed to start the dancing. Each of us is supposed to ask a guy to dance because it's our birthday." Jean's eyes glowed. "And I'll ask someone else to dance. Tom McKay will be sorry he was ever born he'll be so humiliated!"

Jessica and Lila burst out laughing, and Cara gave Jean a big hug. "That's a great idea," she said warmly. "I think that'll do for a substitute pledge task, don't you guys?"

Sandra cleared her throat. "That isn't fair," she said quietly.

Everyone stared.

"What do you mean?" Lila demanded, irritated.

"A rule's a rule," Sandra said. "It isn't fair to let Jeanie off when all the other pledges had to do it."

Jean's eyes blazed. "Sandy Bacon, how dare you say something like that!" she cried. "You're supposed to be my best friend!"

"Hey, calm down," Cara said. "Sandy," she added, "we've already reached our decision. I don't know what's going on with you two," she added, "but I don't want you arguing over this!"

But as far as Jean was concerned, it was too late. The minute the two girls were alone she exploded. Her emotions had been stretched to the breaking point that night, and she couldn't help feeling Sandra was being disloyal.

"How dare you make a fool out of me in front of everyone!" Jean exploded. "I can't believe anyone would do a thing like this to me, least of all my very best friend!"

"You don't understand," Sandra protested, looking stricken. "Jeanie, I—"

"I don't want to talk to you," Jeanie said furiously, her face pale with anger. "I'm telling you the truth, Sandy. Just keep away from me!"

"Jeanie, I'm sorry," Sandra said, putting her hand on her friend's arm. "Please . . . can we at least *talk* about it?"

Jean glared at her. "I don't really see what there is to talk about," she said coldly. And the next minute she had pushed her way past Sandra and into the crowded living room, leaving Sandra alone, staring miserably after her.

Across the Walkers' crowded living room, Steven and Cara were deep in conversation, ignoring the noisy party around them. "You mean you're really not upset?" Steven asked, staring at Cara.

Cara's dark eyes widened in surprise. "Steve, why should I be upset? I think it'll be a fabulous job. You'd be crazy to give up the opportunity!"

Steven looked at her thoughtfully. "But you were so against it when I first told you about it," he reminded her.

Cara waved her hand dismissively. "Oh, *that*," she said. "Honestly, I was just kind of surprised. Now that I've had a chance to think it over, I really don't mind at all." She stood on tiptoe to brush Steven's cheek with her lips. "I'm going to miss you, of course," she added truthfully, "but I'll get used to it." After a pause she added, "Anyway, it's probably all for the best."

"What do you mean?" Steven demanded.

Cara shrugged. "Well, I don't think long-distance romances are very healthy in the end, anyway. If you stuck around here, we'd probably have dragged on for a long time. This way it'll be a good, clean break. We can both meet other people, become more independent—"

Steven looked horrified. "You mean you think that just because I'm going away for a while we should stop seeing each other?"

"How can we 'see each other' if you're in the

middle of the Pacific? No," Cara said, "this is the best way. Believe me, Steve, you won't regret it."

Steven felt his eyes misting over with tears. "It doesn't sound like you're exactly heartbroken at the prospect," he said sarcastically.

Cara shrugged. "Well, I've got to be realistic, Steve. After all, you didn't ask me what I thought of your plans when you called. You just told me what you were going to do. That means I've got to get used to the idea."

"Well, it sounds like you've gotten used to it a lot faster than I would have expected," Steven said bitterly.

Cara smiled at him. "Come on, Steve. Don't be so dramatic. We'll still be friends!"

Steven's eyes burned with anger. "Like hell we will," he said, storming out of the room and slamming the front door behind him as he left the apartment.

"Wow," Jessica said, coming up behind Cara. "Never a dull moment around here tonight. What's with *him*?"

"Oh, Jess," Cara said, her eyes shining with tears, "I just hope you and Liz are right about this scheme of yours. Because if it doesn't start working fast, something tells me Steve and I are never going to talk to each other as long as we live!"

"Oh, dear," Jessica said uneasily. "I hope we're not just driving him away by acting like none of us care."

"You're not the only one," Cara said miserably.

Feigning nonchalance had been the hardest thing she had ever done, Cara thought. If Steven took the job on the *Bellefleur*, she felt her entire world would end. She was willing to do anything to keep him from going.

She just hoped that the Wakefields were right and that this was the way to keep him here.

Seven

Jean woke Sunday morning feeling confused and unsettled, as if she had dreamed something terrible that she couldn't quite remember. All at once the memory of the previous night's party came flooding back to her. The humiliation of being stood up by Tom, and the terrible way Sandra had treated her. . . .

Jean couldn't believe how Sandra had acted. For as long as she could remember, she and Sandra had been like sisters. They had shared everything. Jean depended on Sandra as she did on no one else. And she had always assumed Sandra was completely trustworthy. Until the night before.

Now she didn't know what to think. Her eyes filled with tears as she remembered the sharp words she had exchanged with her best friend. Surely there had to be some explanation for Sandra's behavior. The sorority wasn't very important, and Tom McKay certainly wasn't, after the way he had treated her! But Sandra mattered more than anyone.

Still, Jean didn't feel that she should be the one to make the first move. She was deeply wounded by Sandra's disloyalty, and she thought it was only fair for Sandra to call and apologize.

In the meantime, she wasn't just going to sit around. She was going to do something about Tom McKay!

An hour later Jean was ringing the McKays' door bell. She had taken special pains getting dressed, finally selecting a pair of linen walking shorts and a Fair Isle cotton sweater. Simple but pretty—the look she guessed Tom liked best. In her arms she carried a bag containing get-well presents: a box of special herbal tea, the latest *Sports Illustrated*, and a best-seller that looked really exciting. She ran the bell again, and Tom opened the door.

"Jeanie!" he exclaimed, staring at her. He was wearing cords and a T-shirt and looked, as Jean had expected, perfectly well.

"Tom, you should be in bed," she scolded, trying to make her voice sound tender and concerned at the same time. She pushed past him into the McKays' foyer. "Honestly! Food poisoning isn't something to mess around with. You're lucky you're alive!"

"Aw . . . it wasn't that bad," Tom muttered, reddening.

Jean shook her head. "It must've been pretty bad if you went to the emergency room," she reminded him. "Come on. Let's go somewhere where you can lie down, and I'll show you the care package I brought you."

Tom laughed uneasily. "My mom's going to come home from the supermarket any minute," he said, stepping back reluctantly as Jean made her way into the McKays' living room.

Jean pointed sternly at the couch. "All the more reason to lie down," she said earnestly. "If your mother's anything like mine, she'll have a fit if she finds you up and around before you're really ready."

Tom sank down on the couch and stared at her. Obviously her visit had surprised him, and he had no idea how to act. *Time to really make him squirm*, Jean thought. *Nothing like a little kindness to make a rat feel guilty!*

"I missed you last night," she said silkily, kneeling next to the couch and staring into his eyes. "I was so worried." She put her hand on his forehead, which felt perfectly cool. "I think you have a fever," she said solicitously.

71

"No, I don't," Tom said. "I mean—I don't think I do," he added hastily.

"When you told me you were in the hospital, I was ready to die," Jean said. "I came so close to heading straight over to the emergency room to sit with you. I probably *should* have, shouldn't I?"

Tom looked horrified. "No, you shouldn't have! I mean, you were right to go ahead and go to the party." He looked at her with total confusion. "How was it? The party? Did you have fun?"

Jean shrugged. "It was OK, I guess. It was part of this pledge season we've been having at Pi Beta Alpha," she added, studying his face closely for a reaction, "but to be honest, I'm not really all that excited about the sorority. I mean, I wouldn't mind getting in, but it isn't exactly a life-or-death issue. The party was kind of boring without you," she concluded, putting her hand tenderly on his arm.

Tom stared at her. "Well, I—uh, I missed you too," he said awkwardly.

Jean got up quickly, her voice changing to a no-nonsense tone as she unpacked her care package. "These are to keep you busy while you're resting," she told him, giving him the book and magazine. "And this"—she passed him the tea—"is to settle your stomach. My mom swears by it."

"Jeanie, I can't believe how nice of you this was—" Tom began.

Jean tossed her head impatiently. "Don't you get it, Tom McKay? I *care* about what happens to you," she said. *Boy, am I ever laying it on thick,* she thought. But Tom seemed to be falling for her ruse. The look on his face was positively pathetic, he seemed so grateful.

"What's this?" Tom demanded, taking a slip of paper out of the magazine.

Jean smiled. "That," she said, "is an emergency number. If you feel rotten or need anything, just call it, and I'll be over right away."

Tom's eyes were shining. "Thanks, Jeanie," he said huskily. "You know," he added, "a lot of girls would react differently than you. I mean, I know I loused up your evening. I couldn't get in touch with you till late; you didn't get to have any dinner—"

"Don't be silly," Jean interrupted. "Honestly, Tom, you couldn't help getting sick, could you?"

He didn't answer for a minute, and Jean couldn't help thinking, *But you weren't sick, were you? You humiliated me in front of the Pi Betas. And I'm going to get even if it's the last thing I do.*

If things went the way she was planning, she could count on one thing: This coming Friday night Tom would be telling the truth when he said he felt sick to his stomach. She was going to make sure of that!

Tom put the *Sports Illustrated* down, a perplexed expression on his face. *Girls*, he thought. *The day I ever understand them . . .*

The way he had it figured, Jean West would have been so angry with him that morning she wouldn't have even given him the time of day. And here she had come all the way over to see how he was feeling. She had brought him presents, kept him company for almost an hour, and just before she left, she had even brushed his forehead with her lips.

I must have it all wrong, he thought, rubbing his forehead. From what Sandra had hinted at at the Tennis Shop, he had gotten the impression that Jean was just using him to get into Pi Beta Alpha. But if that were true, why had she come over to see him this morning? Her standing in the sorority had probably been threatened by his behavior the night before, and she *still* wanted to see how he was feeling. Her attitude toward the sorority impressed him, too. She seemed interested in it but not obsessed. The only possible explanation was the most simple. *She must actually care about me*, Tom thought with disbelief. *She must like me. She wasn't using me at all. I'm the one who was in the wrong, and yet she's trusting and caring enough not to suspect my story!*

By that afternoon Tom was convinced Jean West was the best thing that had ever happened to him. He couldn't wait to see her in school the following day; he wanted a chance to make up for standing her up Saturday night. In fact, he was so eager to talk to her he finally dialed her number.

"Jeanie?" he said eagerly. "It's Tom."

Jean paused for a split second. "Tom," she said. She sounded glad to hear his voice. "How're you feeling? Is the care package helping?"

"It's helping a lot," Tom said. "But I was thinking I might need a little special attention tomorrow. How would you like to have lunch with me?"

Jean laughed. "I'd love to, Tom," she said enthusiastically.

"Great. *I'm* going to surprise *you* this time," he told her.

"OK," Jean said. When she hung up, she was smiling. *That's what you think, Tom McKay,* she thought. From here on in, Tom wasn't going to be doing the surprising. She was. And if her plan worked, Tom was going to be good and sorry the two of them had ever met!

* * *

"Steve!" Jessica cried, rushing out to the patio, where her brother was relaxing in the sun with the Sunday paper. "Look what I've got for you—a bunch of brochures on the Far East!"

Steven sat up on the deck chair, squinting at his sister in the strong sunlight. "Oh—thanks," he said. He didn't sound very enthusiastic.

"I still can't believe you're going to be there in just a few weeks," Jessica said, spreading the brochures out and examining them with great interest. "You know, you're going to be able to get such good presents for everyone. How would you like to buy me a jade necklace in China?"

Steven frowned. "Sure," he said flatly. "I'd love to."

Jessica looked up at him. "What are you going to get Cara? I'll bet she'd love something jade. With her coloring, it would look really nice."

"Cara," Steven said dully, "won't be getting any presents. She and I are breaking up. Haven't you heard?"

"No way!" Jessica said. "Why?"

Steven shrugged. "Apparently Cara doesn't feel like waiting eight or nine months till she sees me again. She seems quite happy with the prospect of saying goodbye to me at the end of the week and calling it quits."

"Wow," Jessica said. "But you can't really blame her, can you? I mean, you'll be having the time of your life. It wouldn't be fair if Cara had to sit at home and be depressed."

"I didn't expect her to sit around and be depressed," Steven grumbled, "but I didn't expect her to be so matter-of-fact about breaking up, either. She acts like it's no big deal, as though what we have together doesn't even matter!"

"Well," Jessica said thoughtfully, "maybe she figures that's how you feel, too. Did you talk to her about your plans to leave school, or did you just drop the bombshell on her when you got home?"

"I called her from school and told her," Steven said. He blushed then, realizing that "telling" was not exactly the same as "talking over."

Jessica shrugged. "It sounds to me like Cara's doing the best thing for you both. You'll have much more fun going away without having to worry about her, Steve. Honestly. You'll meet so many fabulous girls abroad! Cruises are supposed to be so romantic."

"Yeah," Steven said gruffly. "That's just it. I think I may be falling for a lot of romantic hype instead of really doing what's best for me."

Jessica could barely suppress a gleeful shout. It was working! Steven was beginning to reconsider. "Oh, Steve," she said, trying to sound disappointed. "You're not going to back out, are you? I was counting on you to buy me gorgeous presents from all around the world!"

Steven didn't answer. His dark eyes were fixed thoughtfully on the sunlit water in the swimming pool. *If only I knew what to do*, he thought.

The truth was, he had come home with some grave doubts about his decision. In fact, he had planned to talk it over with his parents the first night he got home. But they seemed so negative about the idea that he jumped to the defensive, instantly claiming his mind was made up.

Not very grown up, he had to admit. Now he was having serious second thoughts, but everyone was acting as if he'd already signed the contract. And they didn't even seem to care that much!

He was beginning to wonder what they would say if he told them he'd changed his mind, that he didn't want to drop out of college or sail on the *Bellefleur* after all. He didn't know. One way or the other, though, he had to make his mind up for good. And he had to do it soon.

Eight

Jean was trying to find a book at the bottom of her locker before first period when a timid voice interrupted her.

"Jeanie? Can we talk?"

Jean got to her feet, the retort dying on her lips as she saw the look on Sandra's face.

"OK," she said briefly. "What do you want to talk about?"

Sandra gulped, She hadn't expected Jean to make this easy on her. But she couldn't bear having her friend mad at her. The weekend had been torment for her. At least half a dozen times she had picked the phone up, meaning to call Jean and apologize. She just didn't know what to say. Now, facing Jean, she was still at a loss for words.

"Let's go into the lounge," she said. "It'll be quiet there."

To Sandra's surprise Jean followed her into the brightly painted student lounge and plopped down on a couch.

"Well?" Jean said expectantly, looking up at Sandra, who remained standing.

Sandra swallowed. "This is really hard for me," she began. Jean's expression didn't change, and Sandra decided to try another tack. Her eyes filled up with tears, and her tone became pleading.

"Jeanie, you have to forgive me!" she burst out. "I feel so terrible about what happened Saturday night. I've been in total hysterics all weekend. I fell like I just can't function, knowing you're so mad at me!"

Jean's green eyes were impassive. "Sandy, I just don't understand," she said at last. "I've always figured I could count on you no matter what. Saturday night . . ." Her face clouded over briefly, remembering. "What was the deal, Sandy? Were you purposely trying to sabotage me in front of all the Pi Betas, or what?"

Sandra bit her lip miserably. "I'd never do that," she lied. She shook her head. "Jeanie, I was just afraid they'd all accuse me of favoritism again. Honestly! I've been getting so much pressure ever since I put you up, and I didn't want anyone to think I was trying to make an exception for you just because you're my best friend."

Jean thought this over. "I can see that you wouldn't want to suggest making an exception," she said at last. "But you *didn't* suggest it, Sandy. Lila and Cara did. All you had to do was keep quiet, and everything would have been fine."

Sandra thought fast. "It might've been fine on Saturday night. But once everyone got a chance to think it over, I would've gotten a lot of grief for it. I'm not kidding! You just don't know what it's like behind the scenes," she told her friend. "Once you're a full-fledged member, you'll understand."

Jean sighed. "Sandy, I want to believe you so badly," she said. "I've been pretty miserable since Saturday, too. I've never felt so confused before. I just couldn't figure out why you'd want to screw things up for me."

"I don't!" Sandra cried passionately, tears spilling over. "Jeanie, I want you to get whatever you want, forever and ever! That's what being a best friend means!"

Jean's eyes softened. "Oh, San," she said softly, jumping up and throwing her arms around her friend. "I'm so sorry for doubting you. I was wrong to suspect you, even for a minute. I just didn't realize you're under so much pressure from the other members. I should never have even asked you to put me up!"

Sandra swallowed hard. She couldn't believe Jean was forgiving her so quickly. Jean was taking full responsibility, claiming the fight had been entirely her fault.

That's because Jean's a good friend, Sandra thought miserably. *She's willing to give me the benefit of the doubt—to trust me even when no one else would. She really cares, and she's the kind of warm, genuine person who would stick by me no matter what.*

For the first time Sandra realized the enormity of what she had done. In her unfounded anxiety about Jean pledging the sorority, she had put their friendship at risk. It wasn't Pi Beta Alpha that was threatening Jean and Sandra. It was Sandra who was!

She was so relieved that Jean had forgiven her that she vowed at once to give up her attempt to keep Jean out of the sorority. She just hoped Jean never found out what she had done.

"Well," Jean said, trying to sound enthusiastic, "this *is* a surprise, Tom."

"Do you like it?" Tom asked, studying her reaction as he spread the picnic out on the red-checked tablecloth under one of the big shade trees in front of Sweet Valley High.

This guy is off his rocker, Jean thought with disgust as she sat down. *Who in his right mind would dream of having a picnic right in front of a school? Everyone else must think we're nuts.* No wonder Tom McKay didn't have very many dates. He sure had some weird ideas about what was fun.

"I love picnics," Tom said, passing her a piece of cold fried chicken. "My parents used to take my brothers and me out for picnics at Secca Lake every Sunday."

"No kidding," Jean said, fidgeting uncomfortably on the lawn. Her idea of a lunch date was finding some nice, romantic little restaurant. Eating outside was messy. And people were staring at them.

"We used to get ants in our food, though," Tom said, grinning at her.

Jean laughed despite herself. "I have to tell you," she said, taking a bite of the chicken, "I had a disaster the last time I went on a picnic." She proceeded to tell him about an afternoon she had spent hiking with her oldest brother, Richard. "We were about three hours away from anywhere when we stopped for lunch. We were starving," she reminisced, "and all of a sudden Richard started groping around for the knapsack that had the food in it. Gone!" She laughed.

"He'd left it back in the car. We almost died of hunger before we got back to it."

Tom seemed to find this amusing, and soon the two of them were trading stories about their brothers, trying to see who had experienced greater traumas. Jean started to relax, completely forgetting her plan to get even with Tom. He really *was* easy to talk to, and she found herself remembering how much she had enjoyed the few times they had talked on the phone the week before.

"Hey," Tom said, leaning forward and looking in her eyes, "what are you doing after school today?"

Jean thought fast. She had cheerleading practice, but she was sure she could skip it just this once. Jessica was co-captain of the team and would surely agree Operation Revenge was more important than an ordinary hour practicing routines. She also had to find out her latest pledge assignment. She didn't want to mess anything else up as far as Pi Beta Alpha was concerned! Leslie Decker had had to recite a poem in the middle of the corridor; Janice Young and Becky White had had to steal towels from the boys' locker room, and Amy Sutton had to walk backward for an entire day. Jean was just hoping Lila and Jessica would let her off easy.

"Nothing," she said matter-of-factly. "Why?"

Tom snapped his fingers. "Because," he said, "if you're willing, I want to take you to a place that I guarantee you'll love!"

Tom had mixed feelings as he and Jean drove north of Sweet Valley in the late afternoon sunlight, taking Route 1 up to Crystal Falls.

He liked Jean a lot. In fact, he was feeling something he had never felt before. His heart beat faster when he was close to her. There was no denying that Jean was beautiful, he thought. Her creamy skin was flawless, and her eyes sparkled like two perfect emeralds. But it wasn't Jean's looks that were getting to Tom. It was her liveliness, her sense of humor, her natural warmth. She struck him as genuine and caring, someone who would be loyal forever once her affection had been won.

What worried him was a persistent feeling that they came from different worlds. He couldn't shake the feeling that she was too sophisticated for him, that she was the sort of girl who would prefer a restaurant to a picnic, a night at the theater to a walk on the beach. Tom had to admit he was testing her. He had too much at stake not to find out how she really felt right away, because he knew what he was feeling was serious. He was falling in love with her, and he wanted to make sure they were right for each other before either one of them got terribly hurt.

"Clinton Falls?" Jean said, noticing the sign as they turned off the highway. "What's here? The only thing I know is that there's an amusement park here."

"You guessed it," Tom said, smiling at her. "It's the biggest amusement park in this part of the state."

"I know," Jean said quietly, her stomach turning over. She couldn't believe she had heard him right. Ever since she had been a little girl, she had been terrified of heights. Any sort of ride made her sick to her stomach. She hadn't been to an amusement park in years.

"You like rides, don't you?" Tom said anxiously.

Jean thought quickly. "Yes, of course I do. But what about you, Tom? Are you sure your stomach is ready to be flipped upside down— after Saturday night?"

"Oh, I'm all better now," Tom assured her.

Jean bit her lip. She couldn't imagine anything she wanted to do less than spend the next couple of hours hanging upside down with Tom McKay. This was a million times worse than the picnic, she thought. She must have been crazy to agree to come out here with him for another one of his brilliant "surprises"!

"Actually," Tom said after they had parked the car and paid the admittance fee at the front gate, "there's only one ride I really want to take you on. I'm personally not that crazy about all the really wild ones. But the Ferris wheel here is a real treat. Have you ever been on it?"

"No," Jean said unhappily. Tom took her hand as they wound their way through the crowds toward the Ferris wheel. She had to admit she was grateful. His hand was warm and strong, and little tingles went through her when he tightened his clasp.

Tom bought two tickets, and they joined the line in front of the Ferris wheel.

"I've always been a little scared of heights," Jean confessed, her mouth dry.

Tom squeezed her hand, and looked deep into her eyes. "Do it for me," he said seriously. "I promise you it'll be worth it."

Jean swallowed hard. She had completely forgotten why she was here or what her motivation for seeing Tom McKay was. She was frightened, and she felt that Tom was all the protection she had. The Ferris wheel came to a stop, and she hung onto his hand as they moved forward to get on.

Several minutes later they were buckled into their seat. "Tom, I'm scared," Jean whispered. Tom put his arm around her, pulling her close.

"Do you want to get off?" he asked her. "I'll call the guard, and we can get off right now if you want."

Jean shook her head, coming to a decision. "No," she said firmly. She closed her eyes briefly as the wheel began to turn and they began to climb. "This better be worth it," she muttered, her teeth clenched.

"It is," Tom said. "Keep your eyes closed till I tell you to open them. OK?"

Jean nodded, her eyes squeezed shut. They were climbing higher and higher, and she could feel her stomach turning somersaults. Tom was holding her tightly, though, and to her surprise she didn't feel one bit afraid.

"*Now*," Tom said huskily. "Open your eyes now, Jeanie."

Jean swallowed again. Her eyes flew open, and she gasped, leaning forward with a look on her face that was a combination of awe and delight.

"Tom," she breathed, "this is the most beautiful view I've ever seen!"

The mountain ranges on the far side of the valley were jagged and stark, providing a perfect contrast with the gentle green of the surrounding countryside.

"It's always been special to me," Tom said

huskily. "I sort of wondered whether it would be special to you, too."

Jean turned slightly. She could feel Tom's heart beating against her, and suddenly she realized that this wasn't a game anymore. Whatever had brought her here, this was a real person next to her—someone with feelings, important feelings. Not an assignment from the Pi Betas, not a dare but a real human being.

Right then all she cared about was that they were together. Whatever had brought them together, she was beginning to feel something for him . . . something she had never felt before.

"Jeanie," Tom said, his voice gruff. And the next thing she knew, the Ferris wheel was descending and Tom was kissing her, his lips gentle and warm. His arms tightened around her as he drew her toward him, and she felt as though she didn't ever want to come back down to earth again.

Nine

"Listen, you guys," Elizabeth said to the group gathered around the lunch table, "don't forget about the surprise party at our house this Saturday night for Steve. And remember," she added with a giggle, "it's supposed to be a bon voyage party. Make sure you all act really excited about Steve's plans to sail on the *Bellefleur*."

Cara shook her head anxiously. "I just hope this is really going to work. He's been acting so strange every time I've seen him!"

"That's because he's embarrassed to admit he doesn't want to do it anymore," Jessica told her. "Don't worry, Cara, you won't be losing a boyfriend after all!"

"Speaking of not losing a boyfriend," Lila said, her brown eyes quizzical as she looked at Jean, "you sure have been seeing an awful lot of Tom McKay, Jeanie. Are you sure you're not getting a little carried away with your revenge scheme?"

Jean reddened. "Uh—of course I'm sure," she said, taking a sip of Coke. "I have to make sure he really cares about me, don't I? That's the whole point!"

"Well, tell us what the deal is then," Jessica said. "Have you gotten him to be your date at the dance in the gym this Friday?"

Jean nodded. She just didn't feel triumphant about it, that was all. But she could hardly tell the Pi Betas. "Yes," she said slowly. "He's really looking forward to it. And as I said, Dana and I are going to start off the dancing. So all I've got to do is walk up to the front of the gym, pick up the microphone—and say some other guy's name instead of Tom's."

Lila giggled. "Perfect," she said. "That's absolutely perfect."

"What's going on?" Elizabeth asked curiously. She had been at the party the Saturday night before, but she hadn't heard that Tom had stood Jean up. Nor did she like the sound of the story once Lila and Jessica had explained it all to her. She frowned at Jean, thinking that it hardly seemed fair to get back at Tom in front of the whole school. But she wouldn't have dreamed of saying anything in front of all the other girls.

Besides, she didn't know Jean well enough to intrude.

"It'll be so funny." Jessica giggled, obviously forgetting she had ever liked Tom herself. "Jeanie, that's a fabulous idea. You'll really be getting back at him!"

"Yeah," Jean mumbled. She pushed her yogurt carton away. Suddenly her appetite had vanished. If everything was going exactly the way she'd planned, why did she feel so rotten?

"Jeanie, what is it?" Sandra demanded. She had been watching her friend's face during lunch, and she knew something was wrong. But she had waited until they were alone to bring it up. Now, heading to their lockers together, she urged Jean to confide in her.

"It's nothing," Jean said, forcing a smile. "Honestly, Sandy."

"Come on," Sandra said. "I want to help you if I can." And the funny thing was that she meant it, she realized. She just wished she could take back all the things that had happened recently. What an idiot she had been to fear Jean would ever withdraw her friendship! Each day she was more impressed by Jean's loyalty and more embarrassed by her own behavior. But Jean would get back at Tom and get into Pi Beta Alpha without any trouble now, she reminded herself. And everything would be all right again.

"Well," Jean said, "if you really want to know, it's Tom." ·

"Tom?" Sandra repeated blankly.

"Yes," Jean said bleakly. "Tom. I know you're going to think I've flipped, but I really care about him. And not just as a friend, either."

Sandra's mouth went dry. "Are you—are you sure, Jeanie?" she asked.

Jean nodded, her eyes filling with tears. "I've never been more sure about anything," she whispered. The two girls had reached Jean's locker now, and Jean leaned against it, sighing. "So I guess I'm facing a moral dilemma, huh? Either I make poor Tom feel like a fool in front of everyone Friday night and lose him forever, or I tell the Pi Betas to forget it, and I lose *them*."

This is all my fault, Sandra thought. She felt terrible. She could see the pain in her friend's eyes, and she wanted to throw her arms around her and tell her everything. "Oh, Jeanie, I feel so bad," was all she could think of to say.

Jean shook her head. "Well, it's made me do some serious thinking," she said softly, turning the dial on her locker and opening it. "I mean, I always thought being in the sorority would be fun. But to be honest, it was mostly because I wanted to spend more time with you. I was

94

afraid we were growing apart. I thought if I pledged Pi Beta, we'd have more time together and things would be the way they used to be."

Sandra's eyes were shining with tears. *Tell her*, a voice inside urged her. But she couldn't say a word.

"Anyway," Jean said, flipping her hair off her shoulder, "I guess I've realized that the sorority doesn't mean as much to me as I thought it did. I wasn't crazy about the idea of using Tom to begin with. But I did it—and I feel rotten about that now. The plan to get back at him was *my* idea, and truthfully I'm ashamed I came up with it. But I'm relieved to find that I can't go through with it." She laughed ruefully. "Not even for Pi Beta Alpha."

Sandra's heart turned over. She had never heard anything so warm and generous in her life, and she felt sick comparing herself to Jean. *This whole mess happened because I was jealous and insecure*, she told herself. *It's time for me to start taking responsibility, because until I can be proud of myself, I'll never feel secure around her. It's my problem, not hers.*

But Sandra couldn't face the thought of confessing what she had done. It wasn't just that she feared what the other girls in the sorority would say—at this point, she thought she could face that. But she didn't think she could tell

Jean. Jean had been pledging Pi Beta Alpha in large part to get to spend more time with her—and she'd been trying to keep Jean out!

Sandra didn't know what she could have been thinking of. She just wished there were some way to straighten the whole terrible mess out—before Friday night.

"Hey, what's wrong?" Tom asked, tickling Jean under the chin with a blade of grass.

"Oh—nothing," she said.

They were lying on their backs on the grass in the McKays' backyard, staring up at the sky. Jean couldn't believe how happy she was. A couple of weeks ago she would have thought this would be the most boring thing in the whole world. And here she was, enjoying herself immensely. Tom always seemed to guess her mood, too. But she wasn't going to burden him with her decision about Pi Beta Alpha. None of it seemed very important anymore, anyway.

"You know, it's kind of hard to believe the way things are going between us." Tom said. "Especially since we got off to such a shaky start."

Jean looked at him, wondering if she could risk bringing up what had happened at Cara's party. But Tom confessed before she had a chance.

"I didn't really have food poisoning, you know," he said, rolling over and staring seriously at her. "Don't get mad, but I stood you up on purpose."

"I know you did," Jean admitted, smiling. She put her hand up to stop the questioning look on his face. "Wait a minute. Me first," she said. "I admit it. I was told I had to get you to be my date to Cara's party as part of my pledge task. And I feel awful about it," she added. "Really awful. Except that it brought us together, so I guess it wasn't all bad!"

Tom hugged her, but his blue eyes were perplexed. "But how did you find out I didn't really have food poisoning?"

"First you tell *me* why you stood me up."

Tom groaned. "You may not like this," he said, "but your friend Sandra was the one who tipped me off."

Jean stared at him, flabbergasted. *"What?"*

"I knew you wouldn't like it." Tom sighed. "Look, I feel terrible about it all now because I know how much you count on her. Who knows?" he added. "Maybe it was just an accident. But"—he frowned— "she came into the shop on Saturday afternoon, and I got the impression she really wanted to let me know something about the party. It was a bizarre conversation all the way around. But she dropped just enough hints so I became convinced you were just using me to get into the sorority."

Jean was staring at him, her face drained of color. "I can't believe it," she whispered. "*Sandy . . .*"

"Maybe I made a mistake," Tom said uncomfortably. "Maybe I just read too much into it."

"No." Jean said miserably. "I don't think you did. You see, that's how I found out you weren't really sick. Sandy suggested that I should check out your story—in front of all the other girls. So they made me call the hospital."

"Oh, Jeanie, I feel terrible," Tom said, putting his arms around her as she began to cry.

"She must have some reason," Jean said, fighting for control. "I don't know what it could be, but I can't believe she'd want to hurt me on purpose."

"She doesn't deserve you," Tom said, wiping away her tears.

Jean shook her head. "She's my best friend," she whispered weakly. "I've got to give her the benefit of the doubt."

She made two decisions then and there. She wasn't going to tell Tom about her plan for revenge. It would only hurt him, and now that she knew she couldn't go through with it, it was pointless.

And she wasn't going to confront Sandra, either. She loved Sandra, and she couldn't see what good it would do to tattle on her to the other Pi Betas or to accuse her to her face.

She had no idea why Sandra would have wanted to keep her out of the sorority, but she felt it was up to Sandra to tell her about it if and when she felt ready. Meanwhile, though, she couldn't help feeling as if her entire life had changed in the last couple of minutes.

"You look so sad," Tom said tenderly, tracing the outline of her jaw with his finger.

"I guess I feel like I've lost my best friend," Jean said softly, tears filling her eyes.

And as Tom tightened his arms around her, she began to cry in earnest.

Ten

Elizabeth was hurrying down the crowded main corridor of Sweet Valley High, her mind filled with last-minute plans for Steven's bon voyage party. She had so much to do that week she couldn't believe it. On top of everything else, she had to proofread her "Eyes and Ears" column that afternoon so she could get it to Penny Ayala, the editor-in-chief of *The Oracle*.

The door to the student lounge was open, and Elizabeth ducked inside, thinking this was as good a place as any to work in peace and quiet. It was Thursday lunchtime, and the lounge was deserted. Throwing her book bag down on a cushion, Elizabeth got right to work. She barely noticed when the door opened a few minutes later and Sandra Bacon slipped in.

"Oh, Liz," Sandra said, sounding disappointed. "I didn't think anyone would be in here."

Elizabeth looked up from her work and smiled. "Come on in," she said. "I promise I won't disturb you, Sandy. I've got to rush this column to Penny."

"Oh," Sandra said, sitting down uneasily. "You mean the 'Eyes and Ears' column?"

Elizabeth nodded. "Why?" she asked. "Do you have any good gossip for me for this week's column?"

Shaking her head, Sandra reddened. She had been hoping Elizabeth wasn't going to say anything about Tom and Jean. Sandra was feeling worse than ever about her friend. She wished she could screw up the courage to tell Jean everything that had happened.

"No," she said slowly, "I don't have any gossip, Liz."

Elizabeth looked at her thoughtfully. "You know, Sandy, I've been thinking about what Jeanie was telling everyone at lunch yesterday, and I have to admit I'm kind of surprised. Not that I really know Jeanie that well, but I never thought she'd be the sort of girl to take something out on a guy. Especially not without finding out his side of the story."

"You just didn't understand," Sandra said, more angrily than she had intended. Elizabeth looked surprised. "I mean, it isn't Jeanie's fault," Sandra went on. "Jeanie would never hurt anyone intentionally! She's one of the sweetest, most thoughtful—" The lump in Sandra's throat kept her from finishing her sentence.

"Well, that's what I always thought, too," Elizabeth said. "So why is Jeanie planning to embarrass Tom in front of the whole school tomorrow night? That doesn't seem very nice to me. He'll be crushed!"

Tears welled in Sandra's eyes. "I'm telling you, Liz, it isn't Jeanie's fault." Sandra's gaze dropped. "Just believe me; Jeanie isn't to blame," she said hoarsely. Then she jumped up and ran out of the lounge, slamming the door behind her.

Elizabeth stared after her in disbelief. "Boy, did I ever say the wrong thing," she reproached herself, shaking her head as she went back to reading her column.

She had no idea what was bothering Sandra these days, but from the way their conversation had just gone, she guessed it wasn't a good idea to criticize Jean's scheme in front of her.

Elizabeth had seen loyalty before, but Sandra was really going a little overboard!

"Aren't you early for class, Sandy?" Mr. Collins asked with a smile. "It isn't that I don't think English is a great subject. But I always figured you guys kind of liked having your lunch hours to yourselves."

Sandra tried to smile but couldn't. Ordinarily Mr. Collins was one of her favorite teachers. Young and handsome, he resembled Robert Redford. He was a demanding teacher but made the subject come alive. Outside of class he was a great listener—and had a wonderful shoulder to cry on.

That day, however, Sandra couldn't muster any enthusiasm for anything. All she could think about was what she had done to Jean. She felt as if the whole world looked black. She couldn't imagine joining Jean in the cafeteria. It was too hard being around her. Jean was so forgiving about everything, and it made Sandra feel even worse.

"Hey," Mr. Collins said, sitting down on the edge of his desk and crossing his arms. "I have the distinct impression something's bugging you."

Sandra's eyes filled with tears. "Mr. Collins," she said suddenly, "suppose you'd done something rotten—I mean *really* rotten—to someone you care a lot about. You probably never would, but just suppose you had. What would you do about it?"

"Hmmm," Mr. Collins said, his blue eyes

thoughtful. "Well, in the first place, Sandy, don't be so quick to assume I don't know how you feel. I *have* done some rotten things to people I love in the past, and since I'm human, something tells me I might again."

Sandra stared at Mr. Collins. She couldn't imagine the kind-hearted teacher being mean to anyone, let alone someone he loved, but she knew he wouldn't lie to her.

"I guess my own way of handling guilt depends on the situation," he continued slowly. "I mean, it depends on what I've said or done, whether it's reparable, how close I am to the person I've hurt—all those things. But generally I'd say that if there's a chance of righting the situation, I'd try hard to do it. And I suppose, in most situations, I'd tell the person I hurt that I was sorry."

Sandra gulped. "But what if the person didn't know that you'd hurt them?"

Mr. Collins frowned. "That's a tough one, I'm afraid. Can you give me any more particulars?"

Sandra shook her head, tears in her eyes.

"Hmmm," Mr. Collins said. "Well, is there any chance this person might find out about the hurtful thing you said or did?"

Sandra nodded.

"Ah," Mr. Collins said. "So you either confess and then apologize, or you wait and hope the person won't find out. That's your dilemma, I suppose."

"Yes. That's it," Sandra said.

"Well, that isn't easy, Sandy. I have a feeling that you know which is the more ethical course, but it certainly isn't the easier one. And it may hurt the person you care for very much, even if you've been big enough to confess. All I can tell you is that secrets don't always stay secrets. Also, I have a feeling this person would be much more willing to forgive you if you came out with it, instead of waiting to be caught."

"Thanks," Sandra said, brushing the tears from her eyes. He had said exactly what she knew he would say—exactly what she had been telling herself all along.

Somehow she had to muster up the courage to tell Jean. The only question that remained was *how*.

"Mom? Dad? Do you think I could talk to you for a few minutes?" Steven asked uncomfortably. Dinner was over, and the twins were upstairs, doing their homework. This was the first chance Steven had found to approach his parents alone.

"Sure, Steve," Mrs. Wakefield said, smiling up at him from her chair in the living room. "Why don't you come on in and sit down?"

Steven perched awkwardly on the edge of another chair, his eyes on the carpeting. "I've been doing a lot of thinking about Mr. Rose and the *Bellefleur*," he said, " and I was thinking . . . well, you guys don't seem opposed to the idea anymore."

"Well, you convinced us it was what you really wanted," Mrs. Wakefield said, putting down the magazine she had been reading.

"You know how seriously we take your plans, Steve," Mr. Wakefield added. "You're an adult now, and it isn't up to us to interfere once you've made up your mind."

"Well, that's just it," Steven said uncomfortably. "You know, there *are* an awful lot of problems involved in leaving school."

"Really?" Mrs. Wakefield said, looking surprised. "Like what? I thought you had it all worked out."

"Well, take medical insurance," Steven said. "I called Bob last night, and he said the ship can't cover me. It'll cost me a fortune just to get a policy to cover me while I'm at sea."

"Steve, medical insurance isn't the end of the world. Your mother and I could help you out with a loan if you really need it," Mr. Wakefield said, unperturbed.

"And then there's the whole question of my future," Steven added morosely. "What happens if I don't like the ship? I might have a hard time getting readmitted to school. And without a college degree these days, I could really be cooked when it came time to getting a real job."

Mrs. Wakefield raised her eyebrows but said nothing.

"Well, what do *you* think?" Steven cried, anguished.

Mr. Wakefield cleared his throat. "Steve, we feel that this has to be your decision. We're behind you whatever you decide, but you're a grown man now, and we can't make your decisions for you."

Scowling, Steven got to his feet. "I can't believe it," he muttered. "A guy comes to his family to talk over the biggest decision he's ever made, and what does he find? No one's willing to help him. Not even one little bit!"

Mr. and Mrs. Wakefield exchanged anxious glances as Steven stormed out of the room. "Goodness, I do hope we're doing the right thing," Mrs. Wakefield said in a concerned voice.

Steven didn't hear her. He was on his way upstairs, his eyes burning.

A few minutes later he had gotten through to Cara and was sprawled across his bed, the receiver against his ear.

"Now, don't forget we have a dinner date Saturday night," Cara said. She giggled. "Who knows when I'll see you again, so you'd better be on time!"

"Cara," Steven said suddenly, "do you really think I should take this job on the liner?"

A brief silence met his question. "Well," Cara said, "if it's what you want—"

"But what about what *you* want?" Steven demanded. "Don't you want me to stay?"

"Of course I do, silly," Cara chided him. "But I can't expect you to make your whole life revolve around me, can I? If you really want to see the world, I think the job sounds terrific."

Steven felt tears of frustration burning his eyes. He wished he hadn't gotten himself involved in this mess in the first place.

He didn't want to go anymore, that was for sure. The way everyone had been acting convinced him of that. They acted as though they couldn't wait until he was gone! If he really *did* go, they would probably all forget him in a matter of weeks. *Mom'll probably turn my room into a library or something. I won't have any place to stay when I come back to town. . . .* Steven couldn't believe how close he'd come to ruining his life.

And Cara and his family were willing to let him do it! Well, Steven decided, he wasn't going to let their indifference blind him to the fact that leaving college now wouldn't be the best thing for him in the long run.

The very first chance he got, he was going to tell them that. Not, he added to himself self-pityingly, that it really mattered. They probably wouldn't even care what he did!

Eleven

"Jeanie!" Mrs. West called upstairs. "Tom's here!"

Jean took a deep breath and ran her hairbrush one last time through her ebony hair. She knew she looked good that night. Her black dress was the exact color of her hair, and it showed off just enough creamy skin. Little diamond studs in her ears and a strand of pearls around her neck created a dramatic effect. She knew most people would be dressing in black to go along with the spooky decorations the dance committee had set up in honor of Friday the Thirteenth. And for once Jean didn't want her dress to set her apart. She wanted to blend with everyone else.

"Tell him I'll be down in a minute!" she called back, dabbing a bit of perfume on each wrist.

She wanted to keep her composure. It was her birthday, but she wasn't feeling festive. She felt that that evening was going to be a disaster.

At last Jean was ready, and she hurried downstairs to meet Tom. Her heart skipped a beat when she saw him. He looked so handsome. He was wearing a dark blazer and khaki pants. His hair was still wet from the shower but neatly combed. His blue eyes lit up when he saw her.

"Jeanie!" he exclaimed, stepping forward. "I brought these for you," he added, thrusting half a dozen red roses into her arms. "Happy birthday," he added gruffly, leaning forward to kiss the tip of her nose.

"Oh, Tom," Jean said, a lump in her throat. "They're gorgeous!"

Jean's heart was thumping loudly as she arranged the beautiful flowers in a vase. She didn't know how she could ever have dreamed she'd be able to pay Tom back in public tonight. It made her sick, knowing all the Pi Betas would be waiting for her to choose someone other than Tom for the first dance. They would all be waiting . . . and when she couldn't go through with it, that would be it. She'd be cut from Pi Beta forever.

Jean sighed. If only she could sort through her complicated feelings and understand how she really felt! She had made her mind up about the sorority. Or *had* she? Why did she still feel so disappointed at the prospect of not being a member?

Every time she thought about Sandra, Jean got tears in her eyes. She missed her best friend terribly. The few times they had spoken that week had been strained and uncomfortable. Now that Jean knew what Sandra had done, she could barely look at her without wanting to demand why. She had told herself she wasn't going to confront Sandra, but she found that she couldn't act as if everything were perfectly fine, either. She felt stiff and awkward around her, as if they were strangers.

Well, tonight Sandra will get her wish, Jean thought, standing back to inspect the flowers. *For some reason she didn't want me to get into Pi Beta. And the way things have worked out, she's going to have it her way.*

Jean knew there was no way she could go ahead with her plan. Not now.

"Why are you so quiet?" Tom asked gently a few minutes later as he backed his father's car out of the Wests' narrow driveway.

Jean shrugged, a lump in her throat. "No reason," she said softly. "I'm just thinking, that's all."

"You look so beautiful," Tom said. "I still can't believe you're really my date tonight, Jeanie. I feel like I'm the luckiest guy in the world."

Jean bit her lip, her eyes filling with tears. She was remembering what she had said to Sandra the previous week about being lucky ever since she had pledged Pi Beta. *Well, I sure don't feel lucky anymore*, she thought sadly. *I feel about as unlucky as a person whose birthday falls on Friday the Thirteenth should!*

But she didn't want Tom to know how she was feeling. At least she had him.

She had lost Sandra, and she was about to lose Pi Beta. But no matter what else went wrong, she still had Tom.

"Jeanie, are you ready?" Lila whispered, grabbing her by the arm. "We've all been frantic. We were afraid you weren't going to show up."

"Well, here I am," Jean said flatly.

"And you're all set to ditch Tom?" Jessica demanded, joining Lila by the side of the gym.

Jean opened her mouth. "Uh, yes, I am," she said. She just couldn't go into the whole story. It would be simplest to act as if she were still planning to embarrass Tom and then to claim she had just chickened out when the moment finally came.

She looked around her in a kind of daze. The school gym had been transformed by the dance committee. Black crepe paper and forbidding-looking moons festooned the walls; papier-mâché black cats perched on the table where punch was being served, and eerie music was playing. Students had to pass under a big ladder to enter the gym, and the decoration theme of unlucky objects was carried out everywhere. There was a good turnout. Students were pouring through the gym doors, most dressed in black, and all in high spirits, ready for a wonderful evening.

Suddenly Jean stiffened. She had just seen Sandra come in, and her throat ached. If only she could go up to Sandra and beg her to explain why she had done it!

Sandra looked up and met her gaze, and for a moment Jean was convinced her friend's eyes were shining with tears. But it must have been the lights, she decided, because Sandra turned and walked away as if she hadn't seen Jean at all.

Caroline Pearce, the slender redhead who was head of the dance committee, was getting up on the dais with a microphone to begin the evening. Everyone clapped as she tested the sound system.

"OK, folks, welcome to Sweet Valley High's Friday the Thirteenth party!" she exclaimed, and the applause swelled. We're going to start the dancing off by asking two very special girls to come forward and choose dance partners," Caroline explained. "Dana Larson and Jeanie West, could you both come up here, please?"

Tom stared at Jean. "What's this?" he asked her, looking surprised.

Jean pressed his hand. "Don't worry," she said reassuringly.

"You know about this?" he asked, obviously wondering what was going on. She hadn't told him that she and Dana would start off the dancing. It just hadn't seemed that important now that she knew for sure he was the only dance partner she wanted!

"Dana and Jeanie are both Friday the Thirteenth babies," Caroline explained. "They are both celebrating their birthdays today! So tonight we're honoring them. And they're honoring *us* by choosing partners and starting off the spookiest dance in Sweet Valley history!"

Everyone cheered wildly. Jean could see a knot of Pi Betas standing in the front of the crowd. They were watching her expectantly, and when she caught Lila's eye, Lila gave her the victory sign. Jean bit her lip and looked away.

"Dana, you start," Caroline instructed. A fast-paced dance record was put on in place of the eerie music, and Dana took the mike from Caroline and said "Jerry Novak" in a loud, clear voice. Everyone cheered. Dana was the lead singer for The Droids, Sweet Valley High's own rock band, and Jerry was her latest boyfriend.

"OK, Jeanie," Caroline said, passing her the mike.

Suddenly Jean felt dizzy. She could see the expectant smiles on the Pi Betas' faces. Across the circle she could see Tom, looking at her with a mixture of confusion, nervousness, and affection. Then her gaze picked out the face she had been looking for. Sandra was standing just to the side of the other sorority girls. Her face was pale, and her eyes were very big as she stared at Jean.

Jean looked straight at her, and a dozen conflicting thoughts went through her mind. She couldn't really sort out what she was thinking, but she knew what she was feeling. She was feeling affection—affection more intense than any she had ever known before. *Love*, Jean thought with a lump in her throat, *is the only thing that matters*. "Tom McKay," she said into the microphone. A gasp came from the corner where the Pi Betas were standing, but she ignored it. She moved forward across the dance floor, and Tom met her halfway, taking her into his arms, a smile on his face that made her eyes swim with tears.

"I can't believe it," Lila said. "What's she doing?"

"She chickened out," Jessica said with disgust. "Tom doesn't deserve her."

The next minute the girls of Pi Beta Alpha were in a furor, criticizing Jean for having led them on and insisting she be dropped from the pledge list for good.

"First she screwed up last week at Cara's and now this," Lila said with disgust. "Forget it. She's had it now."

Sandra felt her eyes blaze with tears. "But it isn't her fault," she said suddenly, her heart hammering wildly. "It's mine!"

Everyone turned to stare at her.

"Sandy, don't try to defend her," Lila said, putting her arm around her. "I know you must be really disappointed, but she obviously isn't Pi Beta material. Not after tonight."

Sandra shook her head. "That isn't what I mean," she said clearly. Now that she had started, she couldn't stop. "I mean it's all my fault. I tried to keep Jeanie from getting in. I told Tom she was just using him, so he stood her up. She tried to go through with the revenge plan, but she fell in love with Tom. *I* got her into this mess, and I'm the one who should be punished, not her."

"Sandy, what are you saying?" Jessica exclaimed, horrified. "Why would you want to keep Jeanie out of Pi Beta?"

118

Sandra burst into tears. She didn't notice that the music had changed and Jean's dance had ended. "I don't know why," she wept. Jean approached behind her, but Sandra, oblivious, kept talking. "I was so jealous of Jeanie. I figured she had everything and I had nothing, except Pi Beta. I guess I was afraid everything would be over if she got in. And I couldn't stand it. But you can't keep her out! Let her join, and kick me out instead."

Lila and Jessica stared at each other. The other sorority members murmured to each other, clearly baffled by what Sandra was saying.

"Please," Sandra begged, her face streaked with tears. "I'm the one who deserves to be kicked out. This past week Jeanie's taught me a lesson about what it means to care about someone. She wouldn't have hurt Tom tonight for the world. I just wish I could say that I'd treated her with that much consideration."

"Oh, Sandy," Jean cried.

None of the other Pi Betas said a word. They just watched in amazement as the two girls threw their arms around each other, laughing and crying at the same time and looking as though nothing would convince either one to let go.

Twelve

"I can't believe how terrible this week has been," Sandra said, wiping her eyes. She and Jean were sitting on the bleachers in the gym, away from the loud music and dancing. "Honestly, Jeanie, I've never known what it felt like to be guilty before. I just wanted to confess to you so badly, but I felt I couldn't, like once I'd gotten myself into this whole mess I was just stuck."

Jean shook her head. "The thing I still don't understand, though, is why you thought Pi Beta would jeopardize our friendship."

Sandra sighed. "Well, this isn't easy to admit, but I was jealous of you, Jeanie. I felt that everything you did was perfect and everything I did was just sort of so-so."

Jean's green eyes looked startled. "How can you possibly say that? Sandy, *you're* the one who's so smart, who's got such a good sense of humor! And you're so pretty, too."

Sandra thought for a minute. "I guess the point is that I shouldn't have been trying to measure myself against you. I can see how it happened, because we've always been so close, like sisters. And sisters are bound to feel a little rivalry once in a while."

"True," Jean conceded. "But I still don't see how Pi Beta fits in."

"Well, the way I saw it, Pi Beta was the only thing I had that you didn't. OK, it sounds crazy," she admitted with a laugh, "but I honestly felt that way. I dreaded the pledge period for weeks, and when it finally came up, I felt trapped. I knew that the feelings I had were wrong, but I couldn't help having them."

Jean looked at her imploringly. "Why didn't you tell me? If you had just come to me then and let me know how you were feeling, none of this would have happened!" She looked across the darkened gym at the spot where Lila and Jessica were standing with a group of Pi Betas. "I'm afraid we're both out of the sorority now." She smiled.

"I don't care," Sandra said fiercely. "All I care about is that you forgive me. I know I should've come to you sooner, but I just couldn't.

It wasn't until this week that I realized I couldn't keep quiet any longer."

"Well, that's the next thing I wanted to ask you," Jean said. "What made you tell Lila and the others? You could easily have kept quiet, you know."

Sandra sighed. "It was you," she said. "You and Tom. I guess the way you felt about him showed through almost right away. I watched you, I listened to you, and I realized that you were behaving the way you were out of love. And I felt ashamed of myself. I felt like I was being taught a lesson."

"Oh, Sandy," Jean said, throwing her arms around her friend again.

"Hey," Sandra said in a low voice, "it looks like the entire sorority is about to maul us!" She couldn't help giggling as she watched the wave of girls crossing the gym floor toward the bleachers. It was hard to believe she had cared so much about Pi Beta Alpha. All that really mattered was that she and Jean had made up. The rest seemed insignificant.

"Jeanie," Lila said, coming forward out of the shadows, "we want to apologize to you for what you've gone through this week. Pledge season is supposed to be tough, but not *this* tough! And we think it's unfair that you should be cut just because Sandra interfered. We'd like

123

to ask you to join Pi Beta Alpha right here and now, for good."

Jean smiled. "Thanks, Lila, and all of you. That's really nice of you. But one of the reasons for wanting to join Pi Beta was to spend more time with Sandy. I'm afraid I wouldn't be very interested if Sandy's going to be asked to leave."

Jessica, Cara, and Lila exchanged glances. "Well, we talked that over, too. We have a feeling that Sandy's been punished enough already. We're not going to ask her to leave the sorority."

"OK, then," Jean said, smiling at Sandra. "I think you've got yourself a new member—and an old one, too!"

"You're incredibly lucky, Sandy Bacon," Lila whispered as the other girls walked back to the dance area. "A lot of other girls wouldn't have been half as forgiving!"

Sandra didn't say anything at first. "You're right," she managed at last, her eyes shining with tears. "I sure am lucky."

She was watching Jean cross the dance floor toward Tom, and her heart filled with love and pride. Jean West was the best friend in the entire world, and Sandra vowed then and there that no matter what happened, she would never jeopardize their friendship again.

*　　*　　*

"I can't believe it," Jean said, looking up into Tom's blue eyes. They were dancing together to a slow song, one of the last of the evening. "Sandy and I are friends again, and I got into the sorority after all! This is one of the luckiest Friday the Thirteenths I've ever had."

"Really?" Tom asked huskily, drawing her closer. "Funny you should say that," he added teasingly. "It doesn't seem that special to me."

"You goof." Jean giggled. "Don't tell me you're not feeling lucky too."

"It all depends," Tom said soberly, his eyes suddenly serious. "It depends on what you say if I tell you I think I'm falling in love with you."

Jean's heart turned over. "Oh, Tom," she whispered. She rested her head on his shoulder, smelling the clean scent of his after-shave. "I think I'm falling in love with you, too," she whispered.

Tom was quiet for a minute. "In that case," he said, putting his strong hand under her chin and tipping her face up to gaze into her eyes, "I feel like the luckiest guy on earth, Jeanie West."

Jean didn't know what to say then. But it didn't matter, because the next minute Tom was kissing her gently on the lips. Anything she could possibly have said was summed up in the magic of that lingering moment.

*   *   *

125

"Hey, Liz," Enid said, sipping punch as her green eyes focused attentively on two boys across the crowded gymnasium. "Who's that guy with Aaron Dallas?"

Elizabeth squinted, trying to get a good look. "I don't know," she admitted. "I've never seen him before." Catching sight of her twin approaching, she said, "Let's ask Jess. If she doesn't know, no one will!"

"Doesn't know what?" Jessica asked, ladling herself a glass of punch.

"Who the mystery man with Aaron is," Enid said, pointing across the gym.

"Oh, *him*," Jessica said, her eyes twinkling. "Of course I know who he is! His name is Jeffrey French. He's new. He just moved here from Oregon. And," she added merrily, "he's starting school on Monday. He's a junior. He and Aaron met at some soccer camp in Northern California last summer. And he's—"

"Whoa!" Elizabeth cried, laughing. "See what I mean?" she added to Enid. "You ask Jessica who someone is, and she gives you his whole life history!"

Enid didn't say anything for a minute.

"Jeffrey French," she repeated, a funny little smile on her face. Jessica had already moved away with her punch glass, but Enid didn't seem to notice. She was staring across the room at Jeffrey.

"Hey," Elizabeth said, waving her hand in front of her friend's face, "are you under some kind of spell?"

Enid giggled, embarrassed. "No," she said quickly, turning away. But Elizabeth knew her friend too well to believe her. She had a feeling Enid had been bewitched. And it looked as though Jeffrey French had something to do with it.

Thirteen

"Darn it," Cara said, frowning at her watch. "I made reservations at Tiberino's for eight o'clock, but I just remembered I loaned Jessica my mom's cashmere cardigan Thursday night. Can we stop and pick it up on our way to the restaurant?"

Cara and Steven were in Steven's yellow Volkswagen, parked in the driveway in front of Cara's apartment building.

Steven smiled. "Can't we get it later? I'm starving!"

Cara shook her head. "No, we'd better go now, Steve. I think Jessica said something about going out later. If my mom found out I loaned it to someone, I'd get killed. Please," she added, slipping her arm through his.

"Oh, all right," Steven said. He wasn't in the

best mood, and the thought of having to see his parents or his sisters again didn't excite him.

But Cara was insistent, and fifteen minutes later he parked the car in front of the Wakefields' split-level ranch house. "Should I just run in and ask Jessica for it?" he asked her.

"Oh, let me come with you," Cara said.

Steven shrugged. "OK," he said, opening the car door. Cara tucked her arm through his as they walked up the path, and he couldn't help thinking she was being much more affectionate than she had been all week. *Probably because she figures it's our last night together forever*, he thought morosely. He put his key in the lock and opened the door. "Anyone home?" he called. "That's funny," he said to Cara. The front hall was dark, and the whole house was quiet. "They were all here an hour ago. I wonder . . ."

He walked forward into the living room, Cara behind him, and suddenly lights turned on everywhere, and people jumped out from behind the sofas and chairs. "Surprise!" everyone screamed. Steven almost jumped out of his skin. Fifty people were in the living room, all jumping up and down and shouting. A huge banner ran the width of the room, with "Bon Voyage, Steve" written across it in huge red letters. Steven just stood and stared, and the next minute the twins were on top of him, hugging him and shouting "bon voyage" at the top of their lungs.

Suddenly Steven felt as though he'd had enough. "Thanks a lot, you guys," he muttered, wishing he could escape to his room.

"What's the matter?" Jessica exclaimed. "Aren't you excited about your going-away party, Steve? We've been working on it all week!"

Steve cleared his throat. "It's great," he said flatly. "There's only one problem: I'm not going anywhere."

The twins exchanged glances. "What?" Elizabeth said.

"You heard me," Steven said. "I've changed my mind. I'm staying in college. I'm going to tell Mr. Rose I don't want to sail on the *Bellefleur*."

The twins looked at each other soberly. Only their twinkling aqua eyes gave them away. "Well," Jessica said, "I guess we planned the wrong kind of party, didn't we, Liz?"

"I guess we did," Elizabeth agreed. "Hang on a second, Steve. Maybe this will help." She and Jessica took the banner down, struggled with it for a minute, and pinned it back up—reversed. In huge letters, it read, "Welcome Home, Steve!"

"We figured we'd be ready, just in case." Jessica giggled as her brother stared at the banner.

"You rats," he said. "You knew all along!"

"He's staying, he's staying!" Jessica shouted. The guests went wild, and the next minute the Wakefields were fighting over who got to hug Steve first.

"I thought you guys didn't care *what* I did," Steven said, moist-eyed. "I really thought it just didn't matter to you."

"Don't you see, Steve? We *had* to act that way. We wanted it to be your decision, no matter what," Mr. Wakefield said, his arm around his son. "But I've got to admit you gave us a real scare. I'm so glad you've decided to stick with your education."

"Yeah, I guess I just couldn't imagine dropping out when it came right down to it," Steven said. He began to grin as he looked around him.

"Something tells me a lot more underground planning has been going on around here this past week than I could possibly imagine." His eyes sought out Cara's. "Have you been involved in this, too?"

Cara smiled at him and reached for his hand. "I would have died if you'd gone. I could hardly pretend to be behind you, but these two"—she smiled at the twins—"convinced me it was the only way to get you to stay."

"I *knew* you two were at the bottom of this somehow," Steven said.

132

But Jessica and Elizabeth could tell he wasn't one bit mad. In fact, they hadn't seen their brother look this happy since he'd come home for vacation.

"But I've still got one really important question," Steven said, looking serious again. The twins and Cara looked at one another and waited anxiously.

"Is there anything to eat around this place? Cara lured me out tonight with a promise of dinner, and I, for one, am famished!"

The three girls started laughing, and the twins hurried in to get the trays of hero sandwiches and salads they had stashed in the refrigerator.

"We were crazy not to jump at the chance to get rid of him," Jessica grumbled as she staggered under the tray. "Keeping Steve in sandwiches is going to be a full-time occupation tonight!"

But Elizabeth knew her twin was as glad as she was that their plan had worked. She knew the party would be a smashing success, and when she returned to the living room, she was going to give her brother one last welcome-home hug.

At twenty minutes after ten, the door bell rang. "I'll get it," Elizabeth said, hurrying out to the front hall and opening the front door.

133

Aaron Dallas was standing on the stoop, looking slightly sheepish. And next to him was the new boy from Oregon Enid had been eyeing at the dance, Jeffrey French.

"Liz, I'm so sorry I'm late," Aaron said. "I've brought a gate-crasher with me, too, if that's OK. Liz, this is Jeffrey French. Jeff, this is Elizabeth Wakefield."

"Come on in," Elizabeth said warmly. She smiled at Jeffrey, who was even handsomer from this close range. His blond hair had a bright sheen, and his eyes were a dark green. "Welcome to Sweet Valley," she said, putting her hand out to shake his.

"Thanks," Jeffrey said. His voice was surprisingly low and warm, and Elizabeth decided then and there that she liked him. "Believe me, I feel welcome already," Jeffrey added. "The Dallases have been unbelievably nice to me. Aaron's been showing me around. We met at soccer camp last summer, and poor guy—he never suspected I'd show up in town one day, taking him up on his offer to give me the grand tour!"

"It's been a lot of fun," Aaron protested. "We're late because I took Jeffrey over to meet the coach," he explained to Elizabeth. "Jeffrey's exactly what we need on the team. Unfortunately when the coach gets enthusiastic it's hard to stop him."

"Well, I'm glad you made it, both of you," Elizabeth said. "It'll be good for you to get a chance to meet some of the people here, anyway." She smiled at Jeffrey. "Why don't you come on in and introduce yourself?"

"I'd love to," Jeffrey said, his green eyes twinkling. Elizabeth took his jacket and moved to the hall closet, a smile playing about her lips.

She knew one guest in particular who was going to be more than happy to be introduced to Jeffrey: Enid Rollins was going to be overjoyed that the new boy had dropped by.

And for her friend's sake, Elizabeth hoped Enid was one of the first people he said hello to!

Enid has stiff competition for Jeffrey French's attention—none other than Lila Fowler. Jessica and Elizabeth enter the hottest matchmaking duel ever, in Sweet Valley High #31, TAKING SIDES.

SWEET VALLEY TWINS

Tell your kid sister, your sister's friends and your friends' sisters ... Now they can all read about Jessica and Elizabeth in SWEET VALLEY TWINS—a brand new series written just for them.

You love reading about the Wakefield twins, and the whole gang at SWEET VALLEY HIGH. You love the real-life thrills and tender romance on every page of ever SWEET VALLEY HIGH book. Now there's something new and exciting—it's Francine Pascal's latest series—SWEET VALLEY TWINS. These are the stories about Jessica and Elizabeth when they are just twelve years old, as all the Sweet Valley excitement begins.

SO PASS IT ON!
SWEET VALLEY TWINS
is coming soon!

**BEST FRIENDS #1—*Available in August.*
TEACHER'S PET #2—*Available in September.***

SWEET VALLEY HIGH

☐	25033	DOUBLE LOVE #1	$2.50
☐	25044	SECRETS #2	$2.50
☐	25034	PLAYING WITH FIRE #3	$2.50
☐	25143	POWER PLAY #4	$2.50
☐	25043	ALL NIGHT LONG #5	$2.50
☐	25105	DANGEROUS LOVE #6	$2.50
☐	25106	DEAR SISTER #7	$2.50
☐	25092	HEARTBREAKER #8	$2.50
☐	25026	RACING HEARTS #9	$2.50
☐	25016	WRONG KIND OF GIRL #10	$2.50
☐	25046	TOO GOOD TO BE TRUE #11	$2.50
☐	25035	WHEN LOVE DIES #12	$2.50
☐	24524	KIDNAPPED #13	$2.50
☐	24531	DECEPTIONS #14	$2.50
☐	24582	PROMISES #15	$2.50
☐	24672	RAGS TO RICHES #16	$2.50
☐	24723	LOVE LETTERS #17	$2.50
☐	24825	HEAD OVER HEELS #18	$2.50
☐	24893	SHOWDOWN #19	$2.50
☐	24947	CRASH LANDING! #20	$2.50

Prices and availability subject to change without notice.

Buy them at your local bookstore or use this convenient coupon for ordering:

Bantam Books, Inc., Dept SVH, 414 East Golf Road, Des Plaines, Ill. 60016

Please send me the books I have checked above. I am enclosing $_____
(please add $1.50 to cover postage and handling). Send check or money order
—no cash or C.O.D.'s please.

Mr/Mrs/Miss _____

Address _____

City _____ State/Zip _____

SVH—11/86

Please allow four to six weeks for delivery. This offer expires 5/87.